Magical Girl Raising Project
restart
II
Asari Endou
Illustration by
Marui-no
W9-CYZ-566

PECHKA

Can create really delicious food.

CLANTAIL

Can transform the lower half of her body into different animals.

NONAKO MIYOKATA

Can make friends with any animal.

RIONETTA

Can manipulate dolls with her thoughts.

MAGICAL DAISY

Can shoot lethal Daisy Beams.

NOKKO

Can change the feelings of those around her.

GENOPSYKO YUMENOSHIMA

Can block any attack with her magical suit.

SHADOW GALE

Can power up machines by modifying them.

@MEOW-MEOW

Can trap things inside paper talismans.

MASKED WONDER

Can change any object's weight.

PFLE

Uses a magical wheelchair to race at intense speeds.

AKANE

Can cut anything she sees.

LAPIS LAZULINE
Can use gems to teleport.

CHERNA MOUSE
Can make herself really big.

DETEC BELL
Can talk to buildings.

MELVILLE
Can change her color at will.

KEEK
Can do whatever she wants within her personal cyberspace.

3

Asari Endou

Illustration by Marui-no

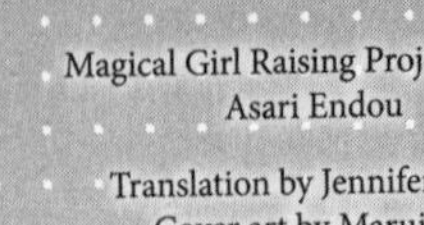

Magical Girl Raising Project, Vol. 3
Asari Endou

Translation by Jennifer Ward
Cover art by Marui-no

Yen On
1290 Avenue of the Americas
New York, NY 10104

Visit us at yenpress.com
facebook.com/yenpress
twitter.com/yenpress
yenpress.tumblr.com
instagram.com/yenpress

First Yen On Edition: March 2018

Yen On is an imprint of Yen Press, LLC.
The Yen On name and logo are trademarks of Yen Press, LLC.

The publisher is not responsible for websites
(or their content) that are not owned by the publisher.

Library of Congress Cataloging-in-Publication Data
Names: Endou, Asari, author. | Marui-no, illustrator. |
Keller-Nelson, Alexander, translator. | Ward, Jennifer, translator.
Title: Magical girl raising project / Asari Endou ; illustration by Marui-no ;
translation by Alexander Keller-Nelson and Jennifer Ward.
Other titles: Mahåo Shåojo Ikusei Keikaku. English
Description: First Yen On edition. | New York, NY : Yen On, 2017–
Identifiers: LCCN 2017013234 | ISBN 9780316558570 (v1 : pbk) |
ISBN 9780316559911 (v2 : pbk) | ISBN 9780316559966 (v3 : pbk)
Subjects: | CYAC: Magic—Fiction. | Computer games—Fiction. |
Social media—Fiction. | Competition (Psychology)—Fiction.
Classification: LCC PZ7.1.E526 Mag 2017 | DDC [Fic]—dc23
LC record available at https://lccn.loc.gov/2017013234

ISBNs: 978-0-316-55996-6 (paperback)
978-0-316-56018-4 (ebook)

1 3 5 7 9 10 8 6 4 2

LSC-C

Printed in the United States of America

Magical Girl
Raising Project

CONTENTS

What Is *Magical Girl Raising Project*? vii

Chapter 6 NEGATIVE AND POSITIVE ... 001

Chapter 7 LAZULINE'S DREAM ... 033

Chapter 8 NOTHING LEFT ANYMORE ... 055

Illustration by MARUI-NO
Design by AFTERGLOW

Chapter 9
THE CHILDREN
093

Chapter 10
PECHKA IN CREATUREWORLD
119

Chapter 11
AND ET CETERA
159

Epilogue
189

What Is *Magical Girl Raising Project*?

☆ Simple and fun for beginners, yet deep enough to keep experts addicted!
★ Features Magical Trace System controls that feel just like real life!
☆ Amazing, ultrarealistic graphics!
★ An ever-increasing library of items to get your collector's spirit burning!
☆ Completely free to play! No purchase required—ever!

Magical girls, welcome to a world of swords and fantasy!

We're relaunching *Magical Girl Raising Project* as a mobile game specifically for magical girls. In this game, you will take on the role of the Evil King.

All those around you are enemies you must defeat. Hide your true identity, scheme in silence, and pursue your goal. You'll need strength, kindness, knowledge, and courage, or you'll never be able to win, even if you are the Evil King—because being the Evil King does not confer upon you any special abilities.

There's only one thing that makes you different, and that's your condition for completion of the game. Turn the tables on the reckless and foolhardy and bring peace to the world of evil.

- Objective: to kill all other players
- Completion reward: ten billion yen
- Area unlock award: one million yen
- Participation award: one hundred thousand yen—received even in the case of a game over

CHAPTER 6
NEGATIVE AND POSITIVE

☆ **Detec Bell**

"Never ye stop! Chaerge!"

Melville's voice behind the girls pushed them out of their frozen stupor, and with near-perfect synchronicity, they all leaped into action.

Keeping her shield between herself and the dragon, Nokko moved into position to protect Genopsyko and @Meow-Meow as she beat out the fire on their bodies with her mop. Behind her cover, she turned on her magical phone and used recovery items on the pair lying motionless on the ground.

Detec Bell ran, silently praying that the dragon would not come her way. She'd been told that the solid weight of the Shield +5 in her hands and the shining blue water charm hanging from her neck would keep her safe, but that explanation wasn't enough to convince her terrified heart.

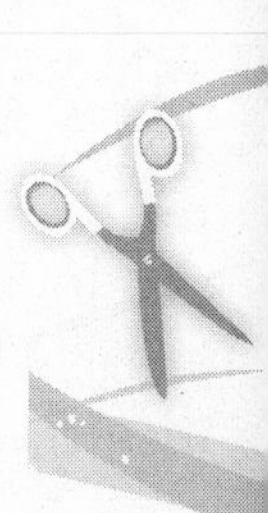

Ahead, Lapis Lazuline blocked the dragon's flames, but the

violent impact was too much for her shield to absorb, and it drove her to her knees. The remnants of the flames danced on the flagstones, close enough to nearly bowl them over with the waves of heat. Rionetta ran past them on the right, Nonako Miyokata on the left, as the dragon's fire-breathing rampage grew even more aggressive. One of the jets rocketed toward Detec Bell, and she hunkered down on one knee with her shield tilted up at a forty-degree angle from the ground.

She bit back a curse. The fire was igniting everything it could reach—the fringes of her cape, the ends of her ribbon, the hem of her skirt—and even leaping to her hair as well, producing sparks. The awful stench of scorched protein reached her nose despite the cavern's moldy smell. Her skin was burning. It was hot—so, so hot—and painful.

Detec Bell couldn't tell what had happened to her left eye, but her eyelid wouldn't open. Under the shelter of her shield, she activated her magical phone to use recovery medicine on herself, praying all the while that no more attacks would come her way. Her role was supposedly escorting the others into battle, so it was funny that she was pleading to be spared when she should have been playing decoy. But still, reason and emotion are two different things, and the pain she was experiencing just then was affecting her emotions considerably. The survival instincts underpinning her fear warned that she couldn't afford to get hit again.

Someone cried out. Though Detec Bell felt like she was about to die, she looked toward the scream's source and found Clantail, her lower body transformed into a grasshopper, collapsed on the ground near the platform. The dragon's thick, long tail was whipping up a gust of wind. It looked like Clantail had attempted to leap high onto the circular platform, but the tail had flung her off.

A javelin pierced the dragon's tail, and several scales flaked off. Blood gushed from the wound. The bodily fluid, resembling muddy red mucus, was flowing toward Detec Bell.

The dragon rose from where it lay, onto all fours. The injury had enraged it. The creature was big enough already, and this just made it look even more imposing. A mere glare from its golden eyes paralyzed Detec Bell with terror. It glared at Melville but didn't attack her. She was behind the red line—the flames and claws wouldn't reach her.

The dragon turned to the fallen Clantail and spat flame.

Clantail held the Dragon-Killer dagger. It was fair to say that their fates were riding on whether she could hit the dragon. And the dragon wasn't targeting Melville, who'd attacked from outside its firing range. It had deliberately sought out Clantail and gone for her. That didn't seem like a coincidence. Was it just instinct? No. The dragon's cheeks were pulled back. Was it smiling?

Detec Bell was shocked.

They'd discussed their strategy right here in this cavern, right in front of the dragon. They had assumed the monsters had hardly any intellect and so wouldn't be able to understand human language, either—despite the fact that none of them could have known for sure.

But then, right as the flames left the reptile's mouth, a blue glimmer arced through the air and rolled to a stop just ahead of Clantail. Lapis Lazuline, her shield raised, blocked the flames. The fire continued with a second and third shot—Detec Bell ran toward them, as did the other girls, but they didn't make it. After the third breath, Lapis Lazuline was blown backward, tumbling away until the rock wall forcibly stopped her. Her arms dangled limply, unable to hold up her shield as she slumped against the wall.

The dragon inhaled a breath to finish off Clantail, collapsed behind Lazuline, but then it paused, its cheeks bulging. Its target was gone. Lips pressed tight against the pressure in its cheeks, it looked around, but Clantail wasn't to be seen. Before the dragon could find the target for its attack, a javelin pierced its throat, and the aimless column of fire disappeared just before the red line.

The dragon reared on its hind legs and howled, burying the malice and intelligence Detec Bell had glimpsed, revealing its bestial nature, roaring until the cavern trembled. Cracks ran up the rock walls, stalactites crumbled, and the rope ladder swayed wildly. The roar might have damaged human eardrums, or even knocked a human out with a concussion. Even a magical girl like Detec Bell felt her knees nearly give way.

She looked up at the rearing dragon, and the ceiling beyond it caught her eye. Something was holding on up there. It was faintly gray, sparsely flecked with color, and had a long tail. The five toes of each foot were splayed wide, sticking fast to the ceiling. It was a gecko.

If Detec Bell remembered right, hundreds of thousands of ultrafine hairs grew on those toe pads, producing a unique attractive force between them and any object they touched, and causing the gecko to cling…or so she had read in some article on an Internet news site or something. Clantail, her lower body transformed into a gecko, hid from the dragon's howl and softly dropped down from the ceiling. In her right hand, she grasped the dagger.

The Great Dragon, roaring to intimidate its enemies and also, most likely, to embolden itself, was so loud that it didn't notice the attack from above. Clantail thrust the dagger into the dragon's crown, and a few seconds later, the earth shuddered below as it fell. Though it had been stabbed by a mere dagger, a large volume of blood gushed from the Great Dragon's head, and its head and forelegs tumbled forward as it collapsed.

Even now, Detec Bell's knees wanted to tremble, but she forced herself to run toward Lazuline, who was still leaning motionless against the rock wall.

Two hours later, a sudden gust of wind swept through the burned stench choking the underground cavern. Looking up, Detec Bell saw light slanting in through the hole in the ceiling. The air must have blown in from there.

The blood smell that had filled the place only moments ago was already gone—not because the wind had carried it out, but because the Great Dragon's body, the source of the odor, had vanished. Monster bodies vanished a set amount of time after their defeat. The dragon was gone, as was its viscous red blood, and only the reek of everything it had charred remained. Though the monsters' bodies would go, the players' bodies did not.

Detec Bell had investigated every single spot she could: the carved rock walls, the tiled flagstones, the curved red line on the flagstones, the circular platform over twenty yards wide in the center of the red circle, the rope bridge hanging above the platform, and the hole leading beyond. She couldn't sniff out anything suspicious on the floor, walls, or elsewhere. Detec Bell sighed. She had even thoroughly examined the dead magical girls' bodies. It had made her sick just to look, but still, she'd closely and carefully mobilized all the knowledge at her disposal. Though her inspection wasn't really reliable enough to be called an autopsy, she had examined them anyway.

A set of footsteps echoed across the stone floor of the massive cavern, which had once fit a great, fifty-foot-long creature with room to spare. The sound gradually got louder, then stopped.

"So, any results?" Pfle asked, lighthearted astride Shadow Gale's back.

"Nothing good." Detec Bell shook her head heavily. Genopsyko Yumenoshima had killed @Meow-Meow. While the Great Dragon's flame had been the direct cause of their deaths, Genopsyko's actions had clearly led to that attack.

Had Genopsyko been following them? @Meow-Meow had been at the rear, but they couldn't ask her any questions now. Nokko, who'd been walking second to last, had said she'd checked behind them a number of times, but there had been no sign of anyone following them, or so Detec Bell had thought, which meant that Genopsyko must have been very good at tailing.

If Genopsyko had been following them, then she had to have heard Pfle's explanation at the beginning: that anyone who crossed the red line would be mercilessly showered with the dragon's flaming breath. Those flames had been powerful enough to evaporate a fist-sized rock, and as Rionetta had put it, hot enough to turn you into a "black smudge."

Genopsyko Yumenoshima's magic had been her invincible suit. She had said that as long as her visor was down, she could even jump into a sea of magma and be okay. But for some reason, she had lifted her visor and was burned coal-black to the core. If @Meow-Meow had been cooked like a Kamakura ham, then Genopsyko was charcoal.

She had been carbonized, leaving hardly a trace of her remains. The reason @Meow-Meow was better off had to be because she'd been equipped with the water charm accessory, which gave her resistance to fire attacks. She hadn't used her shield, so the flames had burned her up, but the water charm had still taken effect.

In other words, that meant that Genopsyko had leaped onto @Meow-Meow with no flame-resistant equipment, her visor up and leaving her entirely unguarded, so she could be burned to a crisp. She had been prepared all along to take @Meow-Meow down with her—it hadn't really been an attack. More like forced double suicide.

When Melville, Cherna, and Lazuline had witnessed Genopsyko's actions, they'd also been left a message hinting of a traitor among them. Detec Bell had seen that message herself. Was @Meow-Meow the traitor Genopsyko had been referring to? Had Genopsyko, through some means, discovered that @Meow-Meow was a traitor and killed her in order to stop her? To punish her? To get revenge?

Pfle swept her bangs back and gazed up at the platform. When she reached for her hair, her elbow hit the back of Shadow Gale's head, making her mount yelp. "Does it look like further investigation will benefit us at all?" Pfle asked.

Detec Bell looked up at Pfle. With her bangs out of the way, her eye patch was clear to see. It was in the shape of a little bird, classy and sweet, and somehow silly, too. "I believe I've investigated everything I should," Detec Bell replied.

"All right. Thank you, Detec Bell. Just one more thing, then." Pfle's gaze shifted from the platform to the hole above it.

Two figures were descending the rope ladder from the opening. The boisterous one was Lapis Lazuline. Of all the survivors, she had to have been most seriously wounded, but after her recovery, she was just as chatty as ever. The next one down was Nokko. She was glum, showing no reaction to Lazuline's babbling. Detec Bell sympathized entirely with Nokko's depression. Of course she would be upset.

What *didn't* seem natural was Lazuline's chipper attitude. She had acted as Clantail's shield and ended up badly hurt. One more hit, and she would have died. But despite all that, she was acting like her usual bubbly, loud, idiotic self.

"Could you help bury the two of them?" asked Pfle.

The remark came while Detec Bell was lost in thought, figuring she should hurry up her investigation, and she looked over at the other girl without thinking. She gazed at her for a while, then silently nodded.

☆ Nokko

Except for the girls who were particularly proud of their strength, no one had objected when Nokko said she wanted to dig the graves herself. They looked sorry for her, as if she was terribly tragic and pitiful. Clantail approached her quietly, pulled out her magical phone, turned to Nokko, and did something with it. There was an electronic sound. "Use that."

She spoke so briefly, it was hard to tell, but Clantail had most likely transferred an item to her out of kindness. The word SHOVEL was displayed on Nokko's magical phone.

Nokko used the shovel to begin digging two holes and piling the earth that would cover their bodies. Come to think of it, she'd helped with burials a number of times since Daisy's death. This time, now that they had this shovel thanks to *R*, the big job of digging graves for @Meow-Meow and the others was a lot easier.

"I'm the strongest, so I'll dig the holes," Lazuline said to her, perhaps because she believed Nokko was hurting. Maybe she was trying to be considerate, since @Meow-Meow and Genopsyko, Nokko's two allies, had killed each other, leaving her on her own.

"No…I'll do it," said Nokko.

"You should just leave it to Lazuline and me," Detec Bell said.

But Nokko shook her head at her, too. "I want to do it. I'm sorry, but could I ask you for some stones to leave on top?" She stuck the shovel into the ground.

If a human attempted to dig a hole big enough to bury a whole body in this hard wasteland, the job might take half a day. But

Nokko, though smaller than the others, still had the strength of a magical girl. Quickly and efficiently, she had no trouble breaking into the ground and piling up the earth from the hole beside it.

Nokko eyed the blade of the shovel. There were no chips, breaks, or dents. It was sturdy, and it stood up to magical-girl strength, too.

@Meow-Meow's body was in such a horrible state, it hurt to look at it, while Genopsyko's corpse was difficult to even recognize as a body. Maybe Lazuline had wanted to take over the grave-digging in order to spare Nokko from seeing this.

Once Nokko was done burying the bodies, she packed the dirt back in and made two earth mounds. On top of those, she placed the small, fist-sized stones that Detec Bell and Lazuline had gathered for her. She would use these instead of grave markers. Now there were six graves lined up outside of the wasteland town. *How many more are there going to be?* Nokko couldn't help thinking with a shudder before immediately erasing the thought.

Nokko stabbed her shovel into the ground, wiped her forehead with the back of her hand, and looked up at the sky. The glare of the sun was aggravating. It was scorching and bright, as it was every day.

Lazuline squatted before the graves and put her hands together. "Sorry they're just makeshift graves."

Nokko squatted down too, pressing her palms together and closing her eyes.

☆ Shadow Gale

From the platform, she could overlook the whole cavern.

Detec Bell had been investigating the area, but she was now gone. She had left to meet up with the others trail-blazing in the new area. They would be exploring and beating things up in the next level.

With everyone gone, the cavern felt incredibly lonely. Until all the magical girls had come, the Great Dragon must have just been gazing at these sights the whole time, all alone. It was just a monster in a game, just a lump of data, and though Shadow Gale thought it was stupid to feel empathy for such a thing, even so, she wouldn't have wanted to need to take up such a role.

"You're getting sentimental right now, aren't you?" came a whisper in her ear, and Shadow Gale's feelings evaporated. "But I'm not here to criticize you. Just stop thinking about our friend the Great Dragon," said Pfle.

"Stop reading my mind," Shadow Gale shot back.

"We've known each other for such a long time. I can read your mind as much as I want. For example...you think I act like an old man."

"I mean, you do."

"Oh, but being concerned about the comfort of your desk chair and saving up all your allowance to scour shopping sites for one is normal for a sprightly youth? *That's* more senior citizen–like."

"That's none of your business."

"If you're going to be sympathizing with our dear Great Dragon's situation, then it seems you won't be able to carry out the mission I have planned for you." Her voice lowered. With Pfle on Shadow Gale's back, Shadow Gale couldn't see her face, but she seemed to be speaking fairly seriously.

"What is it you plan to have me do?" Shadow Gale asked.

"It's no great labor, and neither is it dangerous. It will just take some effort. For the first step of your task, go up that rope ladder, if you would."

As per Pfle's instructions, Shadow Gale climbed the ladder. It led to the next area gate. Going up and down the ladder with the added burden of a second person was a rough task. You'd have to be fairly strong, or you'd likely either drop your passenger or fall. Only today, Shadow Gale had had to do it a number of times. *It's a good thing I'm a magical girl*, she thought, and then she realized, *but then, it's precisely because I'm a magical girl that I'm being worked like a dog.*

After they climbed the rope ladder and crawled out of the hole, all around them was a great body of water, without a single ripple to be seen on its surface. To their right was a ledge, and to the left, a rock wall. Both of them looked natural, seemingly untouched. Within this space was the massive underground lake about half a mile in diameter, and the hole led to its shore. It was over thirty feet up to the ceiling, which was bristled with stalactites. The cavern's width aside, it wasn't nearly as tall as the cavern below. The whole area was green, and the lake was a faint blue. It was colder than below and filled with clear, refreshing air. These were the sights intended for powerful words like *sublime* or *mystical.*

The detail of this space was rather excessive and elaborate for just a path to connect the two areas. Shadow Gale was mildly impressed, but she couldn't handle any more griping about her sentimentality, so she didn't let it show on her face as she walked along. Fortunately, no monsters appeared. Was that because the gate that separated the areas was close by?

The boulders here were mossy, perhaps because of moisture from the lake, so she had to pay attention as she walked, or she'd have been at even more risk of slipping than they had been back in those caves in the subterranean area.

It seemed to Shadow Gale that the water in the lake was somewhat on the clearer side, but she still couldn't actually tell what was in its depths. She took the widest possible detour around it, keeping one hand on the wall. Once she'd gone halfway around the lake, she came to a place on the left side where the rock wall was hollowed out. It was the only spot on this floor that looked to have a human touch. There were stairs carved out here, leading up. Shadow Gale was forced to climb the whole flight. She ascended over a hundred yards to reach a thick wooden door, and upon opening that, they finally arrived in the next area.

This area was a library: The endless lines of shelves packed with books continued off toward the horizon. It was the same in the other direction. Wasteland, grasslands, mountains, a city, a subterranean area, and now for some reason, a library.

Shadow Gale lowered Pfle onto a chair at a table and then sat down across from her. Finally at ease, she looked around. This place had three things in common with the subterranean area: It smelled like mold, it was dreary, and there was no sunlight. The chairs made her butt sore if she sat on them for too long, the long tables seemed like they would break if they took a hit, and the floorboards would probably come loose if you ran on them. They creaked whenever she just walked across. Looking up at the ceiling, she saw panels were nailed onto it at a diagonal, probably an attempt at simulating shoddy repairs. Those same repair sites were lined up perfectly at regular intervals, very much like a video game. This would make it the second time they had come to the library area, but no matter how many times they did, the dust was suffocating.

When they'd first arrived here, Pfle had cried, "Amazing!" and taken a book in hand. But then she had discovered that the books were nothing but covers, just blank paper inside. She'd made certain they were only genuine, pure-white paper, even when soaked in water, dripped with chemicals, held over a candle, or sniffed, and Pfle had not even touched the volumes since.

"Then let's check some things," said Pfle. "Boot up the Item Encyclopedia. It's convenient how it records any items the other parties buy. Check which items are purchasable at this area's shop."

A magic carpet. It would fly, just as promised. It could carry at most the weight of an adult man, and the fastest it could go was an adult man's running speed. This game was big, though each area did differ in size. The largest of the levels, the wasteland, had to be almost two hundred miles from end to end. Ultimately, the magical girls typically got around by running, so a vehicle that could only go as fast as a running man was unnecessary. Aside from Pfle, who had lost her wheelchair, none of the other magical girls would need it.

The holy charms. These were of the same category as the charms sold in the subterranean area. It endowed the one who equipped it with holy elemental defense, which lessened the damage done by demonic monsters, and similarly, also raised the magical girls' attack power against them. According to the bestiary, monsters like fiends and wraiths spawned in the library area, so these would be important items.

The weapon +7. Of course, it was the evolution of the weapon +5. They were easier to use, sturdier, and more powerful than the +5 weapons. But they were insanely expensive—so expensive you had to beat a hundred normal dragons to buy one. Many of the players had spent almost all the magical candy in their possession to get ahold of one of these.

Shield +7. Some of the girls prioritized purchasing this over the weapon. Aside from those magical girls who had an aptitude for shields—or actually, that was just Clantail—so far, none of them had been equipping them as a matter of course. Why? Because they weren't beautiful. Large, boorish shields didn't suit the kitschy, lovable charm of magical girls. Part of being a magical girl was being inefficient at times, even wearing things that got in the way and made it difficult to move, but always being cute nonetheless.

But now they all knew they could no longer afford to hold on to that doctrine. If they wanted to block their enemies' attacks, the shields worked, and they would help the girls survive.

Pfle scrolled through the Item Encyclopedia. "That's it for the items purchased at the shop. Next, for the items acquired through *R*."

R gave you a random item and cost one hundred candy each time. For such a price, the item acquired was nearly always a map that sold for three candy, and they never seemed to get any other items.

Each time Pfle and Shadow Gale had won rewards for finishing quests and things, they had bought a few *R* and acquired a number of items that were not maps.

A toothbrush set. A very normal cup and toothbrush, with toothpaste, too.

A rubber bow and arrow. It was just a toy. It would stick to whatever it hit with a *thunk*.

Rope for mountain climbing. It was a hundred feet long.

"*Ha-ha-ha!* They're all just regular items!" Pfle had said, and she was right. All they ever got were items that seemed unlikely to help them finish the game. The maximum number for all these items was low—all they got was a bunch of 1 (1)s. These items were rare, but all qualified as everyday objects. Among the items that other parties had won were a pot, utensils, and a shovel, and from what they could tell from the descriptions, they really were all just mundane goods. There were still a number of blank spots on the *R* item list, but they were probably just as ordinary.

"But *this* seems interesting," Pfle said. The Initial Location Switch Device. It was one of the applications. You could choose one area from all those available for the players to appear at when they logged in to the game. In other words, you could choose which area of the game to start from. It was worth the time saved in running around, at least. Just like the travel passes and the map, it was shared among a party.

"I suppose it does?" said Shadow Gale. The Initial Location Switch Device seemed to be unspectacular, though useful in its own right. But no, it really wasn't glamorous. It could save them time, but only once every three days.

Pfle scrolled through the item list to the end, where their reward for completing the unlock mission was displayed.

The Dragon Shield. The Great Dragon's drop item. Equivalent to a Shield +12.

Shadow Gale recalled how, immediately before challenging the Great Dragon, Pfle had been oddly fixated on the reward. She'd grumbled about wanting to keep all the candy and real money to herself, but had been unable to get the others to agree to that, and ultimately had ended up with only the drop item, while they had split the candy and cash evenly. Shadow Gale knew Pfle—Kanoe Hitokouji. From her view, that was incredibly suspicious. Kanoe would not be so attached to the candy, and neither would she have been all that concerned about a mere million yen.

Most likely, she had truly coveted that drop item and arranged it so that she would naturally receive it. Kanoe was very good at pulling off little tricks like that.

"This item will be key," said Pfle.

"I'm sure." It was five plus modifications higher than the shields that could be bought by throwing away every candy in your wallet. Considering how powerful the Great Dragon had been, Shadow Gale wouldn't be surprised to hear this was the strongest shield in the game.

"Now then, as to our strategy moving forward…"

"First, can I ask a question?" Shadow Gale interjected.

Pfle's modus operandi was to just do whatever she wanted and then explain everything afterward, partially to brag. If Shadow

Gale wanted to ask anything, she had to do it now, or she'd be forced to listen to the whole story once it was over, seasoned with a dose of boasting.

Pfle raised her right eyebrow halfway and offered her right hand, palm up, to say, *Go ahead.*

"Maybe @Meow-Meow was the traitor, after all…or at the very least, Genopsyko must have thought so."

"If that were true, Genopsyko wouldn't have had to die herself."

"Do you think differently, miss?"

"Regardless of Genopsyko's intentions…" Pfle placed her magical phone on top of the desk and launched the Item Encyclopedia. After a few swipes, it displayed the Miracle Coin's item description. The number of this item in circulation was at 1 (1). "It wasn't @Meow-Meow who stole the Miracle Coin. Her talismans have been burned up, and her magical phone is now unusable. If she'd stolen the coin, then the circulation number would've returned to zero." In other words, that meant that the one who'd killed Masked Wonder was still shamelessly participating in the game.

"Can I ask one more thing?" asked Shadow Gale.

"What is it?"

"Was it necessary to gather so many people in order to defeat the Great Dragon?" Shadow Gale placed her hands in her lap, leaning forward a bit as she looked at Pfle.

Pfle put her right elbow on the table, resting her cheek on her hand as she looked back at Shadow Gale. This was Pfle: calm, collected, and brimming with confidence. Even just after surviving nearly certain death, she was perfectly composed. "Have you forgotten what a terrible struggle that was? It was only by mustering all our forces that we were finally able to defeat it."

Shadow Gale wouldn't deny that it had been a desperate struggle. It wouldn't have surprised her if even more of them had died aside from @Meow-Meow and Genopsyko. But still, she wondered if those numbers had been necessary. Shadow Gale had thought of a way to complete the mission with fewer people, and more safely—though it had been after they'd already beaten the Great Dragon. Pfle would have probably come up with the same idea.

Besides, Pfle's attitude was strange.

Back in elementary school, Pfle had been hit in the face with a dodgeball, and it had given her a nosebleed. Even then, she'd maintained a calm expression and said, "The rules are that face hits don't count, right?"

And just the other day, though Pfle had made every preparation to challenge Cherna Mouse, she had lost the duel, and her magical wheelchair to boot. Still, she was calm enough to compliment her opponent ("That magic is amazing.") as Shadow Gale carried her on her back. Even when Pfle—Kanoe—failed, she would never scramble to save face. She would act as if it hadn't been a failure, and everyone would be fooled into thinking that she'd never really screwed up.

That battle against the Great Dragon had been a near-failure. They'd accomplished their goal and defeated the dragon, but they had let Genopsyko's suicide attack happen, and @Meow-Meow had ultimately died for nothing. Pfle didn't bring it up, but Shadow Gale felt this reaction was different from her usual show of courage, pretension, and stubborn pride. Shadow Gale couldn't put her feelings into words. But something just felt wrong to her. It was unsettling.

Shadow Gale thought, *Pfle had been expecting something, hadn't she?* Even if what had happened to @Meow-Meow and Genopsyko was not the result of Pfle's actions, she'd still gathered all of the magical girls together, anticipating that someone would take action, and created an ideal situation for that to happen.

Pfle had said that in order to find the culprit, she would examine their characters. If one of them caused an incident, it would be important information for her. Pfle had lured that person into action—telling them to just give it a shot—in pursuit of that major piece of intelligence.

She'd done exactly the same thing once already, when she'd revealed in front of the whole crowd that Masked Wonder had been murdered. That wasn't an announcement that should be made right in the middle of such chaos, was it? Wouldn't it have been better to wait until they'd all calmed down? She'd chosen that moment to drop the bomb, *knowing* that it would rile them up—or rather, so she could see their reactions when they were riled up.

If Shadow Gale was right, then Pfle was part of the reason @Meow-Meow had died.

Only a villain would think of causing an uproar in order to see everyone's reactions. Or even if you did think it, you wouldn't go and carry it out. But Pfle was a villain. Shadow Gale believed she was capable of it.

Once again, Shadow Gale scrutinized Pfle. She was the same as ever, and Shadow Gale couldn't read her face.

Seemingly indifferent to Shadow Gale's inner thoughts, Pfle suddenly opened her mouth. "I've come up with an idea."

"What is it?"

"Let's disband our party."

Shadow Gale's hands nearly slid off her lap. She tensed them and peered at Pfle. Pfle was resting her cheek on her hand, smiling in enjoyment.

☆ **Pechka**

The next level, closed to them for so long, was the library area. It didn't make any sense at all that the level following the damp subterranean area would be a moisture-abhorring library. Though there hadn't been any rhyme or reason to the order of the areas so far: wasteland, grasslands, mountains, city, and then underground.

Violence was unsuited to libraries. They were founded on a desire for knowledge, wisdom, or other vocabulary associated with learning. It seemed obvious to Pechka that fighting, the antithesis of those values, would be inappropriate in such a place. You could say that even running down the hallways was a seed of violence.

Clantail and the library area did not get along at all. The place smelled old, moldy, and dusty, and the briefest scuffle sent thick clouds of dust into the air. The place was run-down, too. Dilapidated. Running around with a deer body made it too easy to kick through the floor, so ever since they'd come into the library, she'd transformed into smaller animals in order to fight. At first, she'd gone with a deer or a pony, but then, once she'd figured out that four-legged creatures weren't good for fighting within a confined space, she'd generally been taking the form of a largish ape. You'd think an ape would be more humanlike than a four-legged animal, but still, a beast is a beast, and the humanness of it just made Clantail especially frightening. *She really is cutest as a deer or a pony,* thought Pechka.

The library area had some unique features that hadn't been present in the previous area. One had to do with the monsters' traits, while the other was a feature of the area itself.

Nonako Miyokata's dragon charged, sending black mist flying in all directions. A devil took the shape of a lion to attack Pechka, who jerked up her Shield +7. After she blocked three strikes, she rushed over to sit down in a chair. When the lion saw Pechka in the chair, it stopped attacking. Clantail took advantage of this moment to thrust her spear straight through a bookshelf toward it. The lion somehow managed to dodge, and Clantail's spear tore open its shoulder instead. But when the great ape forming Clantail's lower body attacked with another spear, the lion couldn't dodge, and she skewered its torso. It spasmed a few times and disintegrated. Rionetta stretched her arm joints to their limits to slice apart a devil flying through the air, and when the scattered remains of the wraith Nonako's dragon had attacked attempted to rematerialize, Nonako herself stabbed it with her streamer-trailing ritual staff to finish it off.

The library area featured a great variety of monsters—or so they had been led to believe at first, but when they checked the monster encyclopedia, they found that was not the case. There were only three types of monsters in the library area. The reason they had misunderstood was because these enemies could change shape. The base form of one of these monsters looked like a pitch-black angel cut and kneaded from darkness itself. They were called "demons" and "devils," and they transformed into a variety of different animals: lions, leopards, hippos, and elephants, too, and even the dragons they'd fought underground before. Their animal forms were not that threatening in and of themselves. Even Pechka could knock down an angry beast if she put her mind to it. Magical girls were faster, stronger, and tougher than wild animals.

The issue was not that they could transform into beasts, but that they were also fast, strong, and tough enough to be able to match magical girls in a fight while also transforming at will to adapt to the situation. Only with the holy charm, which increased elemental attack and defense; expensive equipment with the +7 modifier; and some cooperation were they finally able to get the upper hand against these foes.

The names "demon" and "devil" indicated two distinct monster types, but they couldn't be differentiated at a glance. They dropped the same number of candies and had the same ability to shape-shift, too. The first one to notice the distinguishing feature was Nonako Miyokata.

"Ohhh! If you look closely, you see their hairstyles are *différent*!"

The demons' hair flipped inward. The devils' hair flipped outward. Their entire bodies were black, so it wasn't really "hair" so much as "the hairlike part," though. There was hard-to-differentiate, and then there was this.

Aside from the demons and devils, there were also wraiths. These were hazy in form, like black mist, and upon closer inspection, one could pick out a faint feminine shape. Punches and kicks would only go through them ineffectively. They could pass right through everything, not just the girls' attacks: floor, ceiling, tables, and bookshelves. But in spite of this, *their* attacks were solid and painful when *they* attacked. These enemies were unfair, attacking without letting their opponents strike back—or they would have been, without the holy charms.

Equipping a holy charm enabled physical contact with the wraiths, making it possible to damage them. Sound and light could also hurt them, but no one in their group had any moves like that, so they used an uncomplicated method of attack.

With the holy charms, they could leave the wraiths to Nonako's pet dragon, since they weren't that strong, while the magical girls would go for the devils and demons. Pechka focused on defense. This became their basic strategy in the library area.

The most notable feature of the library area was that it had safe spots. To be precise, no one sitting on the chairs within the building would be attacked by enemies. If you sat down on a chair when things got dangerous, the monsters would stop their onslaught. For a magical girl who wasn't all that good at fighting, it was a welcome option. Checking to see if there was a chair in the area before each fight as they explored became habitual not only to Pechka, but to all of them.

It was also nice that, unlike in the other areas so far, they could have a calm meal here. As long as they sat politely in chairs, they could relax and devote themselves to eating.

Pechka got the pot out and filled it with a stack of stones and rocks from the subterranean area and rested her palms on them for five minutes to transform them into a delicious meal. The menu for today was hashed beef.

"Like, that thing, *t'sais*. That demon. It was just like Clantail, how it transforms and stuff," Nonako said, still chewing. That was not an observation Pechka would ever give voice to, even if she was thinking it. When she silently looked over at Clantail, she saw the other girl wordlessly spooning food into her mouth. Currently, Clantail was a girl's upper body attached to the body of an ape where the neck would be. She was frighteningly tall, even more so than when she was part horse. She came off as that much more intimidating.

Generally, when they were eating, the smell circulated at the same height as the food. With Clantail towering above the rest of them, it disturbed the aromatic current where she sat, and somehow this bothered Pechka. She couldn't help but be concerned about the smell of the food she'd made.

"When I first saw you, Clantail, I thought, 'Oh! I have to make that my *bébé*.' I was even disappointed when I found out you were a magical girl. It's the same with that demon, *t'sais*?"

It was pretty rude to be saying she was just like a demon, wasn't it? And Rionetta didn't scold Nonako for it, either. She was enthusiastically devouring her hashed beef.

Apprehensively, Pechka looked at Clantail. She couldn't see any emotional reaction. The ape, lacking any part equivalent to a horse's tail, just sat solidly with its hands on its knees. Clantail had set two chairs side by side and placed her large ape rear on both, but they still looked like they might collapse at any moment.

"The demons can transform into *animaux*, so I thought it could be my friend, but no. These *monstres* are a disappointment."

Beside Nonako, her dragon was scarfing down its hashed beef atop a line of three chairs. Entirely focused on its food, it showed no concern at all for the implication that if its master had been able to make friends with a demon, the dragon would have been doomed to dismissal.

Like the dragon, Clantail, having been treated much like a monster, showed no sign of anger or upset, and wordlessly finished her hashed beef before she laid down her spoon and pressed her hands together. "Thank you for the food."

"It was *délicieux*! You're amazing, Pechka!"

"This is the reason I can keep a stiff upper lip through all these stinky, sweaty battles," said Rionetta.

Pechka smiled shyly in response to her party's praise, tugging on the decorative feather on her hat. No matter how many times these compliments raised her spirits, she couldn't get used to it.

Their meal ended, and when they were about to head out for more grinding, their magical phones rang with an alert.

An event is now occurring. Players, please gather in the wasteland town square.

Pechka felt oddly chipper. Rionetta's sharp tongue had stopped just short of causing a serious fight, Nonako was cheerful, and Clantail didn't seem to be annoyed. That may only have been because she didn't have any hooves to tap to express her irritation, but Pechka doubted it.

It had been a shock when Genopsyko Yumenoshima took @Meow-Meow down with her in the Great Dragon's cavern. But considering the reasons it had happened and reaching a conclusion had lessened the impact.

Pechka had heard that earlier, Genopsyko had come to Detec

Bell's party and left them a note hinting at the existence of a traitor. Next, Genopsyko had taken @Meow-Meow down with her to be burned up in the dragon's flames. Logically, her motives would point to @Meow-Meow being the traitor and Genopsyko punishing her for it, right?

They were being forced to play a game where one wrong move would spell their deaths. That fact had not changed. But Pechka felt less anxious in spite of this because the one recognized to be the traitor had been eliminated, the monsters in the library weren't that strong and dropped relatively large sums of candy, and it seemed that the next level would be the location of the final battle. They'd discovered a message in the library area that read, *The Evil King's castle is next.* Since it was called the Evil King's castle, their ultimate foe had to be there. And if the Evil King was there, it would be the final level—since the goal of this game was to beat him.

It made Pechka feel better to know that their objective was close. Having a goal in sight enabled her to enjoy the marathon more than she would if she were unsure how far they had left to run.

The premaintenance event in the wasteland town square was not a cruel and unusual one—such as *Whoever has the fewest magical candies dies*—but rather a light, peaceful, typical one: It was a rock-paper-scissors tournament among all the girls, and the winner would receive a thousand magical candy. No matter who you were, a thousand was nothing to sneeze at. You'd have to defeat ten demons to gather up that much.

"I'm sure you've all noticed, but from this area on, the items sold in shops will all be expensive, pon. You often won't have enough candy for the items you want, pon. Furthermore, some items will have only one or two in circulation, so there won't be many, pon. Please try to earn a little more candy to acquire the items you want ahead of the other players, pon," Fal said all at once, before taking a big breath. "Though I think it would be best if you could decide who gets which items through peaceful conversation, pon."

At the end of a fierce and even contest with Lazuline, Pfle won the rock-paper-scissors tournament.

"It sounds as if there will be a shop in the Evil King's castle as well, hmm?" said Rionetta.

"*Oui*, and it'll be selling some pretty expensive items, too."

"Let's leave one of Clantail's spears as a +5, then. If there are weapons with even more plus modifications on sale in the next area, it will be a major financial loss."

"*Oui, oui.*"

"Um," said Pechka, "once the next area is unlocked, it might be best to look for the town as soon as possible, huh?"

"Indeed," Rionetta agreed. "You've heard what Fal said? Whoever buys items first is victorious, it seems."

As Pechka discussed the upcoming area with her party, she glanced around at the other groups. Shadow Gale was rushing out of the square, while Pfle, sitting on a magic carpet, watched her go. It seemed that the two of them were going to be working separately. At some point, Melville had disappeared. Was she acting solo?

Detec Bell called out to Pfle, and the two of them clustered together with Lapis Lazuline and Nokko, discussing something. Since @Meow-Meow and Genopsyko were dead, Nokko was without a party, and it looked like she'd be joining up with them. Pechka wasn't in a position to be worried about anyone else, but she'd been concerned about Nokko, so she was relieved that another party would take her in.

Nokko was the kind of girl you wanted to protect when you looked at her. The effect was so strong that even Pechka felt that way toward her. Nokko was all alone, fidgeting, and needy…or so it seemed. If there was another group that would take her in, that was for the best. Pechka breathed a sigh of relief.

But with Pfle, Lazuline, Detec Bell, and Nokko all together, didn't that mean Shadow Gale was not just off doing something else, but rather entirely out of the party? It seemed that there'd been some reorganization going on while Pechka's attention had been elsewhere.

She shifted her gaze back to her own group. Rionetta and Nonako Miyokata were talking, and Clantail was nodding. Theirs was the only party that had remained the same since the start of the game. Pechka felt her logic was selfish, but the death of someone she had hardly spoken with would be totally different from the death of one of the party members she'd been working with to complete the game. Though she'd gotten off on the wrong foot with them, they were all her friends now, and they were important to her. She didn't want Clantail, Rionetta, or Nonako Miyokata to die.

Pechka pressed her thumb into her palm and squeezed it tight.

☆ Nokko

Returning from the game to real life, Noriko resumed her daily routine. Though it was the same three-day span, it didn't feel like it at all.

Noriko came home from school and immediately dropped her backpack there before she went straight to the hospital. She could have gone from school to the hospital, but if she were still wearing her backpack, her mother would look unhappy. It was more efficient to leave her backpack at home, get her mother a change of clothes, some basic items, money, and other necessities, and take those to the hospital with her. On her way there, if Noriko saw gloomy people on the street or at the hospital, she would use her magic on them.

Fundamentally speaking, in order for a magical girl to use her power, she would have to be transformed. In other words, you couldn't use magic as a part of your day-to-day routine. But Noriko knew how to make practical use of magic in her daily life. Most likely, this method was only available to her right now.

Nokko looked about ten years old, and Noriko's real age was also ten years old. Not only were the two close in age, Nokko also looked a lot like Noriko. Of course, they weren't exactly the same. To make it work, she obviously had to wear her normal clothes, change her hairstyle, dye it black, and use little tricks with accessories and her facial expressions. What's more, if she fervently believed that she was Nokko Nonohara, she could use Nokko's magic to transmit that belief to everyone around her. All of this made it possible to go about her day transformed into a magical girl so that she could use her powers easily, even in class or while walking home. Noriko was still growing, so she didn't know how long she could keep doing this, but still, she'd use it as long as she was able.

Using magic on a daily basis meant that her powers got much more of a workout than most. It was basically like training. The essence of a magical girl's powers stays the same for her whole life, but in a general way, she could become more proficient with practice. She could activate her abilities faster, and they'd become more effective and have greater range; the area of effect would broaden, and she'd become able to do things that had been impossible for her previously.

You couldn't rest on your laurels after becoming a magical girl. That was just the beginning. Nokko was grateful to that older girl who had once told her that, though she had long since joined the roster of the dead. Her words lived on within Nokko. Using magic repeatedly as a part of her daily life was part of her training.

Nokko had heard of cases where a girl's magic would grow suddenly, stimulated by powerful emotion, but though some might yearn for a life like something out of a *shounen* manga, it was beyond her reach to realize that. Striving for growth through diligent, daily effort, little by little, like building up a stack of rocks, suited Nokko better.

As might be expected from a medical facility that boasted the status of best in the prefecture, this hospital really was large. It didn't have just food stands on its premises, but also convenience stores. Not only did it have things like barbershops and full-scale restaurants, Noriko had been shocked to find out it even had a store for consumer electronics, a bookstore, and a Western-style candy shop. She'd eaten cake with her mother on the hospital terrace once, some type with a name so long she couldn't remember it. It had been written in French, too.

She greeted the doctors, nurses, and patients with smiles, occasionally using her magic, until she knocked on the door to her mother's hospital room. When her mother replied, "Come in," Noriko opened it. Her mother's examination was done by this time, and she was back in her room, about fifteen pages into her paperback.

Noriko told her mother about her day at school, making it sound as fun as she could, and took out an apple, swiftly peeling it. Noriko had taken over the house chores two and a half years ago, so this task was simple for her.

"Listen, Noriko," said her mother.

"What?"

"If you ever have any problems, tell me about it, all right?"

The hand holding the knife reflexively stopped. Noriko looked back at her mother. She'd recovered quite a bit, compared to when she'd been sickest, and her cheeks were beginning to fill out again. But she was still worse than at the start of her illness, and it made her eyes seem especially large. They were looking intently at Noriko.

"Yeah. If anything happened, I'd tell you. If there was anything." Implicitly, Noriko was saying, *Nothing is wrong.*

Her mother was just staring at her.

Noriko thought back on all she'd done since she'd come into the room. Had she been different from usual? Could anything about her have made her mother worry? She might have been acting a little too bubbly. Maybe that ended up being suspicious.

She examined herself and zealously called to mind enjoyable things, transmitting those feelings to her mother in an attempt to dispel her concerns. As long as she had fun things, as long as she had happy things, she would be okay. She didn't want to make her mother worry about her.

She cheerfully bade her mother farewell and then walked down the hallway, the taps of her feet on the linoleum sounding as she thought. Clearly, she was in a dangerous situation right now. But she couldn't tell her mother about any of it. She wouldn't make her worry any more.

Noriko got the feeling that she understood the reason why the master had added this maintenance period—the three days in a row when they would be returned to reality. By forcing them to alternate between their normal lives and the game, the master was trying to make them more attached to life. They couldn't just forget their normal lives as the days in the game rolled by and then go off and sacrifice themselves heroically or something. They couldn't help but recall how they valued their lives and the people close to them.

But even so, Genopsyko had died and taken @Meow-Meow down with her. Noriko couldn't understand what she had been trying to do. And considering what she'd first seen of Genopsyko's character and disposition, it didn't feel right. Would she have chosen to die like that?

Nokko's magic acted on people's hearts. She had always worked with people's emotional cores, paying very close attention to what made them unique, always observing and analyzing everyone around her. Even in the game, she had continued to do that.

The surface personality that Genopsyko had shown them had been the cheerful and fun nerdy type. From what Noriko could tell, she'd kept hidden a seed of arrogance; she was laid-back, possibly to the point of being irresponsible, and careless. Being absolutely safe within her suit, she had said things that seemed somewhat egotistical to Nokko. She was safe, so she wasn't all that fussed about crisis, and that had been what had led to her injury.

This wasn't the portrait of a person who would push up her visor and leap straight into certain death. Genopsyko's personality was defined by her safety. Her idiosyncrasies were built on the fact that she was absolutely untouchable.

Had the samurai girl changed her personality when she cut her up, even though her visor was down, and destroyed that security? Noriko reflected on her own circumstances.

She'd once been part of a family of three. She'd believed that come what may, they'd all stand together in life. But then her mother had fallen ill, and her father had run off. Thinking back on the person she'd been before her father had left, she felt like she'd changed a lot. Perhaps the shock of that battle had changed

Genopsyko's personality, taking her from laid-back magical girl to a hysterical one who would willingly die and take someone with her.

Noriko couldn't say that @Meow-Meow hadn't been suspicious at all. She'd been acting as if she had known something. Perhaps that was part of the reason for Genopsyko's suicide attack. Now that both of them were dead, though, nobody would know.

All of Nokko's party members from the beginning of the game had been lost, and she'd ended up all alone, but fortunately, Detec Bell and Lapis Lazuline had welcomed her into their party. Because of their nature and position as heroines, magical girls would always extend a helping hand to those in need, even when they themselves were in trouble. Nokko was good at looking needy, and in actuality, that image had not been inaccurate since this game had begun.

Most likely, Detec Bell and Lapis Lazuline had invited her to their party purely out of the goodness of their hearts. But Nokko would do well to remain cautious around Pfle. She'd fed them the cliché line that everyone says when they split up with someone after a fight—*Shadow Gale and I had a difference of opinion, so we parted ways*—but she hadn't appeared to really mean it. When @Meow-Meow had died, and when Cherna Mouse had died, and when that samurai magical girl had died, too, Pfle had taken control of the group and assumed a leadership position. Nokko couldn't let her guard down with Pfle.

Even coming out of the game world and going from Nokko back to being Noriko Nonohara, she was still needy. She was in trouble—financial trouble. When she returned home and checked her bank account, she found a fresh hundred-thousand-yen deposit there. The reward for defeating the dragon in the area unlock quest, divided evenly between the ten of them, came to that amount. Apparently, @Meow-Meow had not been counted, since she'd died before their strategy had begun.

The hundred thousand made her glad. Very glad. It was heartening, but it wasn't enough. She needed more money.

MASTER SIDE #6

"That's how I got the idea! If the Magical Kingdom is just gonna leave them be, then someone's gotta do it! We've got to test them to see if they really are the right kind of magical girl. I don't mind playing the villain here—*someone's* got to do it!" The girl cried passionately, spraying spit and banging her fists on the table. The coffee cup and saucer bounced, sloshing the dark-brown liquid. "You get it, right, Snow White?"

The girl in white was still sitting there, unmoving. She didn't nod, shake her head, or open her mouth—she just watched the café au lait vibrate in her cup. Her white magical-girl outfit looked out of place with the cheap folding chair and office desk.

"You get it, right, Snow White? You made it through your trial without killing anyone and buried her, plans and all."

"The Magical Kingdom demands that you release the magical girls." The visitor in white shifted her gaze from her café au lait to the girl across from her.

The girl beamed under that cold, hard stare. "I suppose I miiight comply, depending on your conditions."

"What are your demands?"

"Radical reform of the selection process for magical girls. And

the reforms must be retroactive. Go back to past exams, bring to light the problematic ones, and strip the girls who took them of their certification."

"If this is the same thing you came to the Council before to advocate for—"

"And there will be no compromises or concessions. At all. I'm not changing my mind, and if you won't go with that, then you're giving me no reason at all to release the 'children.'"

"We can't negotiate if that's the case."

"Magical girls are chosen by the gods. We can't have even a smidgen of any impurity among us." She was smiling.

The magical girl in white intently examined that expression. For a few minutes, neither of them spoke. Then, without a word, she stood, pushed the folding chair aside, and turned away from the other girl.

The magical phone lying on the table turned on. "Snow White! There's no time, pon! Six of them are dead already, pon! Please hurry and—"

The mastermind slammed her right fist down onto the magical phone to turn it off, and the shrill synthetic voice coming from the device cut out. "I'll say it one more time: *You'll* understand."

"We will continue negotiations." Her back still turned, the white magical girl spoke quietly. "So don't kill any more."

"What?" With her pointer finger, the first girl adjusted her glasses as they slipped down her face, and her lips twisted. "I haven't *killed* anyone, you know? That thing with Magical Daisy was, well...an unfortunate accident. But once I gathered them together to make them play the game, they just started going right ahead and killing one another. I never told them to, you know? In fact, the rules make it so that they can cooperate. I've given them proper hints about it, too. I've never cheated anywhere. I made this game so that a good, legitimate magical girl will be able to complete it. I'm a kind, *kind* game master for giving the children a chance for reexamination. I mean, they all became magical girls through the wrong method, and properly speaking, they should have been removed without question, riiight?"

The magical girl in white did not reply, putting her hand on the doorknob.

The other girl yelled after her, "You tried to read my mind, didn't you? Did you think that I might have some weakness? Is that why you came here? I'm telling you: I have no weaknesses. Here, I'm invincible. I can do anything, and nothing you do will work. I'm just like a god. One of the other girls from your time was named Nemurin, right? My thing is similar to hers. As long as I'm in this world, nobody can touch me. I have no weaknesses. That's why, even if you do read my mind, it won't bother me at all." It was neither a lie nor an exaggeration that she was invincible as long as she was in this world. If you killed her, she wouldn't die, though you couldn't even kill her in the first place. And she could do anything. "This is actually a private place just for me, but I invited you in specially, Snow White—because I want to make friends with you."

The magical girl in white said nothing in reply to the other girl's patronizing remarks, leaving the room and closing the door softly. The lines of light peering in from beyond the door narrowed bit by bit and finally disappeared.

The girl, though she was now alone, continued to babble on and on. "I've got nothing to be ashamed of. I'm just saying what I believe is right and actualizing how I think things should be. That's why I can let you read everything in my head. If you've seen what's in there, then you must understand, right, Snow White? You and me, we can cooperate. We *should* cooperate, you know? After all, we're both the *right* kind of magical girl."

CHAPTER 7
LAZULINE'S DREAM

☆ **Pechka**

Pechka was looking at her new deposit of a hundred thousand yen, but it didn't excite her like it had before. If someone were to come tell her she could quit the game for a million yen, she would have canceled the time deposits with all her New Year's money in them and gone to her father and grandfather, pleading, *Don't ask any questions—just trust me*, to scrape together the sum. And though it wasn't like her, she might even have been willing to lie and say a bad man had deceived her and gotten her pregnant. She would be willing to raise money through her friends or use her magical-girl powers to do it. Judging from what she recalled of her friends' reactions when they ate her food, she could charge for that, at least.

But these thoughts would never leave the realm of fantasy—because there was no kind benefactor who would allow her to quit the game if she paid a million yen.

Once during their exploration, Pechka had waited until she was alone and then summoned Fal to ask a question.

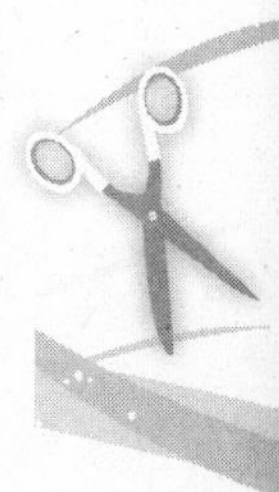

* * *

"Do you mind if I ask you something?"

"What is it, pon?"

"What would happen if everyone refused to play?"

"Um, basically, there's a punishment for any magical girl who abandons the game. The punishment in this case would be, essentially, that her heart would stop, pon. If all of you arranged to quit at once, the whole thing would be deleted...or so I'm told, pon."

"What would happen then?"

"You would drift in this cyberspace forever, never able to return to the real world, pon. So I can't recommend it, pon."

Pechka was crestfallen.

"You're not the first one to ask that question. So...don't be too discouraged, pon."

The way Fal spoke with sympathy somehow made Pechka angry, and she switched off her magical phone.

All their exits had been cut off. They couldn't abandon the game or challenge the master, and they still couldn't send any messages to the Magical Kingdom. They'd also all been reminded that they'd be killed if they told anyone, so they couldn't seek help, either. They had no choice but to head in the direction indicated by the very person who had dragged them into this game: the master.

That was it. Their one sliver of hope: completing the game. The end was getting close. The next area would be the Evil King's castle, and Pechka's party had saved their candy while doing a good job of steadily upgrading their equipment. They'd become quite accustomed to the game's battles, and even Pechka was now competent enough when it came to pure defense with a shield.

If they could just finish the game, it would all be over. If they could just get through this, everything would get better. Pechka prayed for them to remain safe until then, at least, when she pressed her hands together before her home altar like she always did. She went to school and gave Ninomiya his lunch after school in the park. To Chika, her three days of solace flew by like an arrow. She wanted to experience them slowly, make them last just a bit longer, but time would not stop.

She chatted with Ninomiya, sitting alongside him on the park bench lit by the setting sun. He talked about how his coach had instructed him to be more of a team player. He seemed to be reflecting on this, acknowledging that perhaps it was true he often went off on his own and did whatever he wanted, and that he should put in his own best effort while also striving work together with his team. A typical boy of Ninomiya's age would probably feel resentful after such a scolding from a teacher or parent and wouldn't repent like that. Perhaps it wasn't just Ninomiya's talent that was bringing him success in baseball, but also his humility. Chika had thought someone often called a genius would be arrogant and self-centered, but maybe that had just been her assumption.

On the other hand, what about herself? Even if she hadn't necessarily been selfish, it wasn't as if she had done everything she could for others.

Once, in the library area, a devil had attacked Clantail from behind while she was fighting off a demon. Pechka had felt like she'd had her hands full just defending herself, but she still should have been able to call out to her teammate, at least. *Clantail, watch out!* or *There's one behind you!* or something. It would have been enough just to yell something brief. Fortunately, Nonako Miyokata had kicked the devil and Clantail hadn't taken that hit, but she'd been lucky. Clantail could have died because of Pechka's inaction. Just thinking about it made her feel like something was gripping her stomach tight.

Ninomiya told her how his coach had told him it was important to call out to people, and that because he hadn't done so, they'd let a fly ball become a blooper, and the coach had been mad about it for the whole day. Recalling his coach's fury, Ninomiya hugged his arms close, frowning a little, as if he were cold.

That idea that it was important to call out to people could be applied just as well to Pechka. If she had called out to Clantail, there would have been no problem. If it happened again, she wouldn't just defend herself. She'd watch out for her allies, too. If they were in danger, she'd let them know. If it seemed like even shouting wouldn't make it in time...though the idea was horribly frightening to her, she would try to body-slam them with her shield up, at least. As long as she didn't freeze up in fear, she'd do her best.

Ignorant of Pechka's contemplation, Ninomiya talked about how the pitching machine had broken recently. It was now dim in the park, and no more people were walking the streets. A tortoiseshell cat meowed from where it lay on top of the slide.

☆ Detec Bell

Silver grass swayed in the wind. Willows stood in orderly lines along the sidewalk in front of the station. The road was even named simply Willow Street. At the edge of these roadside trees was this lone patch of fluttering silver grass. Nobody had planted it. Had the seeds floated in from somewhere, then? And if so, why hadn't it been cut before it had gotten this tall?

Just the sight of the silver grass brought these questions to mind, but all the people on the street passed right by it. Not a single one stopped. They had enough on their plates worrying about themselves, so they weren't going to consider the grass. Even Detec Bell, who was getting sentimental as she watched the silver patch in the autumn dusk, would normally have been entirely occupied with her own business.

Since Cherna Mouse had died, Melville had left their party, and they had welcomed in the lonely Nokko, as well as Pfle after she'd apparently split with Shadow Gale due to a fight. So once again, Detec Bell was in a party of four.

But though they'd regained their former numbers, they weren't as powerful in battle as they had once been. The new members didn't make up for the loss of Cherna Mouse and her overwhelming size, and Melville, master of the bow and wielder of camouflage magic. Nokko wasn't the battle-oriented type, and Pfle was even worse now that she'd lost her wheelchair and was using the magic carpet to get around.

Detec Bell had never been all that great at fighting to begin with, either. A detective only needed enough skill in martial arts to be able to keep up with crooks and didn't pursue any extraneous abilities beyond that. She hadn't done anything like specialized training to fight monsters.

Inevitably, their party came to focus on exploration rather than hunting. Pfle gave instructions, Detec Bell used her magnifying glass and other detective tools to discover all the hidden messages and such, and when the time came to fight, Lazuline was their main force. Pfle would swiftly back off to a safe location and give directions, while Nokko would wield her mop and Detec Bell would hold the enemies at bay with her staff. Meanwhile, Lazuline would throw a gem, disappear, reappear, and vanish again to confuse the enemies with her teleportation magic. She would kick, punch, pose, and drop one-liners like, "I am the blue flash that dances on the battlefield: Lapis Lazuline!"

Until now, Lazuline had been overshadowed by Cherna Mouse and Melville, two of the strongest fighters among all the girls, but Lazuline was pretty strong and bold herself. Back during their battle with the Great Dragon, as well, she'd been the one to jump in front of the flames without concern for the danger to protect Clantail, the key to their victory, and this had caused Lazuline to be the most heavily wounded of all of them. Lazuline herself had said, "It was so hot and it hurt so bad, I thought I was gonna die!" But her tone was also light. She didn't see it as all that serious, nor did she boast of her contribution.

Though Detec Bell had no desire to emulate Lazuline, she had to admit that throwing yourself so casually into danger was very much like a magical girl. But that casual and flippant attitude really did bother Detec Bell. Something deep in her heart whispered, *You can't trust her.* She was driven by a hunch that she had to look into Lapis Lazuline.

* * *

The city was where Detec Bell worked as a detective and magical girl. The bustling and chaotic area was well-known enough that everyone out in the country would have heard of it. People flocked here from within the city and without, giving her that much more work as both a detective and a magical girl.

The area Detec Bell stood in now was much like her own home turf, but rather more specialized in certain regards. It was on the outskirts of Tokyo, in a place that had been a post town with a wealth of inns back in the Edo period. Just three steps from a certain JR station most people would recognize, you'd hit the red-light district. Bright neon lights, the suffocating heat of bodies, and the grating din of the crowds made for a stunning atmosphere.

The men's attire presented a wide variety in age, occupation, and class, but all of the women were scantily clad, even in the cold weather. Some were even wearing near-translucent attire with skirts as short as they could get.

Even in such a materialistic and lively district, it seemed there were still old poets who left the silver grass by the roadside trees. It wasn't surprising that a magical girl, bundle of emotion that she was, would make this her haunt. This was Lapis Lazuline's home base…or so Detec Bell figured.

With her girlish appearance, Detec Bell was bound to have a run-in with the law and get dragged to the station by some local cop. Furthermore, unlike the time Detec Bell had tracked down Magical Daisy, she couldn't let Lapis Lazuline catch sight of her in costume. Detec Bell continued her investigation, doing everything she could to keep her form as Shinobu Hioka.

But even as Shinobu Hioka, she was still a young woman. In her long-sleeved casual shirt, a fall jacket, and cotton pants, she looked like she was going out to the neighborhood discount store. Though she was dressed like a local, for a young woman walking around at this hour, it was clearly strange. Plus, her light makeup made her stick out like a sore thumb. She had no choice but to equip herself with clothes, makeup, and accessories from a department store in the next neighborhood over, but she didn't feel like her makeshift costume truly made her blend in among the professional girls. And she was cold from showing so much skin at this time of year, even with stockings on.

Furthermore, even though she was just faking the look, men would occasionally approach her anyway, which made her investigation that much more troublesome. She'd managed to complete her investigation of Magical Daisy within three days, but she wouldn't be able to finish this one in that span of time. This led her to doubt her abilities as a detective, but she wasn't going to give up now. She'd gotten a clue. She just had to rely on it to push onward.

Buildings' memories were different from human memories: They wouldn't disappear, fade, or become vague. Even if their tenants moved, their stores were renovated, or they were altered due to a change in fire alarm or emergency exit regulations, as long as the main bulk of the structure was intact, it would always remember.

Skirting some drunk's pile of vomit, Shinobu walked down a back street, surreptitiously transforming to kiss a wall in search of a building that might know Lapis Lazuline. Avoiding notice and being careful to stay out of sight was a common part of every one of a magical girl's activities. Detec Bell was quite familiar with it.

Along the way, she witnessed a small pickup truck honking its horn as it ran through a pedestrian-only street jammed with people. The driver's hair looked like Charlie Brown's, his face was bright red, and he had a beer can in one hand while his other rested on the wheel. This sight, which might cause one to doubt their sanity, convinced her that yes, there was a lot of work for a magical girl to do in this neighborhood. She walked, and sometimes ran, in search of information.

At first blush, a red-light district and a magical girl seemed incongruous. But contrary to that preconception, they were actually surprisingly compatible. Detec Bell knew this from experience.

In any case, her feet pounded the pavement until she discovered a building that had managed to witness Lapis Lazuline during the last maintenance period. Though they had had only a brief encounter when Lazuline jumped down onto its roof, what was important was that she'd found a clue at all.

Following Lazuline's trail from the building, Shinobu discovered the roof of an office tower that Lapis Lazuline frequently used to rest, as well as a hostess club that had witnessed Lazuline switch back to human form. The people at the club said that she hadn't switched back to her human form inside, but out back in a dark alley that didn't see much traffic. When it informed Shinobu that Lazuline looked like "a young girl," Shinobu's only thought was, *Well, that's no surprise.*

Buildings never forgot, but it was difficult to get human characteristics out of them. They could differentiate between people if you were to show them a photo, but asking for their characteristics in order to create a facial portrait would just be too difficult—Shinobu's artistic abilities aside.

She poked into the cleavage of her thin dress with her index finger to pull out a golden chain with a pocket watch on the end. A day and a half had passed since the second maintenance period had begun. She wanted to uncover Lazuline's identity before they returned to the game, if possible. She didn't have much time. She tucked her pocket watch back in and exhaled a sigh. Her breath wasn't visible yet, but in this season, it would be no surprise for the weather to turn chilly the next day.

"Huh?" called a familiar voice, and Shinobu turned around.

Even in the darkness, the blue of her dress was vivid. White over-the-knee socks emphasized her healthy thighs. Her cape was decorated with fluffy fur, and the pin holding it sparkled with a gem. The black-and-white striped tail that hung from her bottom twitched. Her glossy black hair was cut in an even line at her shoulders, and she had a tiny mole like a teardrop near her right eye.

It wasn't that Shinobu hadn't imagined that she might, in the process of tracking down Lapis Lazuline, encounter the girl herself. She'd been even more secretive with her magic for that reason, taking care to avoid being found not only by regular people, but also by anyone else in her trade. To avoid standing out as much as possible, she had dressed herself in garish clothing and heavy makeup. There was no way she could have been noticed. But still.

"You're Bell, right? Why're ya out in a place like this?"

Shinobu reexamined herself. She was clearly the human Shinobu Hioka and not Detec Bell. But now that she'd taken a good look at herself, she couldn't explain her way out of this. Anyone who would look down at themselves after being addressed as "Bell" could be none other than pretransformation Detec Bell: Shinobu Hioka. *But still,* she thought, *can't I come up with some kind of excuse? Can't I talk my way out of this somehow?* She couldn't come up with anything.

Lazuline clapped her hands in joy. "You're not from round here, are ya, Bell? Travelin'? Oh, but why would ya be goin' on a trip now? Did ya come out just to see me?"

Shinobu hesitated, then slowly nodded.

"For real? Awesome! Ya comin' to hang out with me is the best surprise ever! But wait, how'dja know where I live? Oh, must be 'cause you're a detective. You can do all that investigatin' stuff, can't ya? Oh yeah, you did say ya found out where Magical Daisy lived, huh? Pretty amazin' stuff, Bell!"

While Shinobu was busy thinking about how she would make it through this situation, Lazuline was working herself into a lather. Did she think that Shinobu could find magical girls without any evidence or hint just because she was a detective?

"Well, since ya came all the way here, I'll show ya my place," said Lazuline. Shinobu was startled. That had been her ultimate goal, but she hadn't imagined that Lapis Lazuline herself would invite her in.

Lazuline closed her eyes, raised up a blue gem, and cried, "Lazuline mode, off! Cancel transformation!" and struck a pose as she turned back into human form. There was no need to yell or anything when canceling a transformation, but that was very like Lazuline, in Shinobu's opinion.

"Then I'll show ya the way. Follow me, Belly!"

The girl was wearing a high school uniform—a blazer. She

looked sixteen or seventeen. But everything about her appearance was heavily made-up. Her makeup wasn't like Shinobu's makeshift heavy look; it was properly done: faint blue eye shadow, red lips, mascara that was thick without being clumpy, and white cheeks. Her hair was a maroon-brown color, fashioned into a complicated braided updo.

When Shinobu had been in high school, she'd had fashion-conscious classmates like that, and they had hung out with similar girls. She'd never exchanged any more words with them than necessary. All they had in common to talk about was school, and she'd figured that any conversation with them wouldn't be very interesting.

"Bell! Whatcha doin'? You're gonna get left behind!"

Shinobu dragged her feet behind the teenager in front of her. She couldn't figure out what this girl's goal was. She couldn't understand her train of thought, either. What she did understand was that she was in a bad situation.

From the back alley, they headed into a residential area. When they cut through a children's playground, the teenage girl deliberately walked along the seesaw, crossing over without falling as it tilted under her weight.

She talked to a cat on a stroll atop a concrete wall, asking it, "How ya doin' today?" It meowed in reply, and she answered, "That's pretty nice," before turning around and smiling at Shinobu. She was all dolled up, but she looked innocent at the same time. It didn't seem like she was trying to deceive Shinobu, and she didn't appear to be hiding anything. That alone sent shivers down Shinobu's spine.

"Over there," the teenager said, pointing at a line of apartment buildings. They were all five stories tall, each one assigned a number. Moonlight illuminated their white walls. They weren't fancy—they were typical for an older complex and very standard apartments. Her gait still playful, the girl indicated one of the buildings, marched through a lot containing a smattering of parked cars, and arrived at the entrance.

It wasn't all that far from the red-light district. It hadn't been more than a ten-minute walk from where she had found Shinobu behind that cabaret club. But in spite of that, it was quiet and dark. Also cold. It struck a stark contrast with the heat and desire not so far away. Shinobu's footsteps sounded loud to her, as did her breathing—and not just her own. She could also hear the cheerful inhalations of the girl in front of her.

It was dark, and there was no sign of any people around. Just one step off the path, and Shinobu could probably get away. But even if she were to run now, she would eventually end up meeting Lazuline again in the game. The only difference was whether she'd be cross-examined now or later.

Though this girl was supposedly going somewhere specific, her stride seemed whimsical, somehow—perhaps because of her cat-like nature. She was like the kind of stray you always had to keep an eye on. Despite the late hour, she ran up the stairs three at a time, not even considering that she should walk quietly. Shinobu just barely managed to keep up.

"Welcome to my castle," said the girl.

There was no nameplate. The whole door was pretty old, and the keyhole and hinges corroded by red rust, but it opened and closed smoothly. Had it been oiled, then? The inside of the apartment was neater than Shinobu might have expected—or rather, there just wasn't anything in there.

The girl went down a hall and guided her to a room, where she set out a soft cloth object—some kind of throw pillow or floor cushion. Her host ran off again, feet tapping on the hall floor, and Shinobu was left alone.

It didn't look like she was in the living room. This was probably Lazuline's bedroom, but there was little sign that anyone occupied it. The room was fairly small and featured one big traditional-style chest of drawers, and that was all. The lone furnishing took up about a third of the usable space in the room. Looking around where she sat, Shinobu found nothing else. She stood up to look at the top of the chest of drawers and saw a photo stand. She was stretching up to reach out to the photo when the sliding door was smacked open.

"Sorry for the wait!"

The girl carried two cups filled with black liquid in her right hand, while in her left was a snack bowl full of potato chips. Her right knee was bent, and she was standing on one leg—she'd probably opened the sliding door with her foot. Shinobu panicked and was about to sit back down again when the photo frame fell over with a clack. It didn't kick up any dust, so it had been properly cleaned. It seemed somehow incongruous that this place was so well maintained and clean—even the hinges on the front door had been oiled—despite the fact that it didn't seem very lived-in.

Shinobu cleared her throat and then slowly and deliberately sat back down.

The girl explained, "Daddy has to go out at night for his work, so it's just me at home t'night. Ya don't hafta act shy, Bell."

Daddy. What sort of *daddy* did she mean?

"Oh, and when I say 'Daddy,' I mean he's actually my dad. Don't go imagining weird stuff."

"I wasn't imagining weird stuff." Shinobu felt like this was the first time in a long time that she'd heard her own voice. It sounded hoarser than she'd expected. Maybe because she was so anxious compared to the high school girl smiling broadly in front of her. When Detec Bell sipped the black liquid offered to her, it fizzed and bubbled in her mouth. The chips were consommé-flavored. Consommé potato chips and cola—the girl's tastes were surprisingly down-to-earth, if a little odd.

When Shinobu turned to look out the window, she saw the world below glittering with neon lights. Though the light reaching them seemed so intense, the hustle and bustle had gone away.

"Um..." Shinobu wasn't as hoarse as before, perhaps thanks to the cola. "How did you know I was Detec Bell?"

"I could just tell." The girl's expression said simply, *Why wouldn't I be able to?*

When Shinobu made a face that insisted, *How?* the younger

girl gave her an even more baffled look. Shinobu noticed the teardrop mole under the girl's right eye. It was exactly the same size and position as Lazuline's.

"A magical girl and her regular self seem totally different, but they're similar in some ways. My master beat that stuff into my head enough to drive me crazy."

A burst of laughter escaped Shinobu. Fortunately, there was no cola in her mouth, so she didn't make a mess on the rug. The moment after she'd realized that teardrop mole was in the same place as Lazuline's, this girl had said that. The timing was so perfect, Shinobu couldn't help but laugh.

Holding her stomach, she chortled for a while, repeatedly wiping away her tears, but when she looked back at her host again, the girl's self-satisfied look had turned sour.

"I never said anything funny," the girl said.

"Oh, sorry, sorry."

"My master actually did teach me a bunch of stuff." The girl stood up and reached out to the top of the dresser. She was taller than Shinobu, so she could reach the photo stand without stretching. Of course, inside the frame was a photo. In it, two magical girls stood together, smiling. One was Lapis Lazuline. The other one was half a head shorter than her. The girl's blue hair flowed down to her back, and though she was smaller, her gentle smile made her seem older than Lazuline, who was giving a toothy grin. "This is her."

"You mean your examiner from when you first became a magical girl?"

"No, no. The old Lapis Lazuline."

Shinobu's brow furrowed. She didn't really understand what that meant.

"I'm the second Lapis Lazuline. I inherited the name from the old one."

Each time they hit a point of confusion, Shinobu asked questions, and when their conversation got derailed and sidetracked, she corrected the course until she had slowly but surely gotten the story from the other girl.

Before she had become Lapis Lazuline, she'd been a magical girl under the name Blue Comet. She worked hard at her job, and the old Lapis Lazuline, who'd already gained quite a reputation in the Magical Kingdom by that time, had identified her talent.

The girl said that the old Lapis Lazuline had brought a passionate petition to her—Blue Comet.

She was exhausted, body and soul, she'd said. She couldn't continue being a magical girl any longer, but she wanted the name Lapis Lazuline to live on, as proof of what she'd been. If possible, she wanted the name Lapis Lazuline to be passed on down through successive generations forever. In exchange, she had said she would teach Blue Comet everything she knew as a magical girl. She would make her the greatest magical girl ever, if she would just accept her proposal.

It had been very selfish. Lapis Lazuline hadn't considered how she might be imposing on someone else. And most wouldn't normally agree to such a self-centered request. But Blue Comet was not a regular magical girl. She was destined to be identified as an odd bird. She loved fun and she loved having a good time. If she believed she would enjoy herself, she didn't mind discarding her own name to inherit someone else's.

A magical girl was, generally speaking, not allowed to change her name. The old Lapis Lazuline had used her status and connections to the fullest in preparation for her name to be passed down. And she hadn't just done the legal work. She had trained Blue Comet to be a magical girl who would not bring shame to the name of Lapis Lazuline. She'd hammered knowledge, skills, training methods, philosophy, and various other things that weren't inherent to magical girl–hood into Blue Comet's head. This was how Lapis Lazuline the Second had been born.

Maybe all that talk of special skills and knowledge had been a scam...but Shinobu couldn't say for sure. Back there, she'd just been Shinobu Hioka, but Lazuline had recognized her for who she really was. She never would have been able to do that without the acumen she described.

And so the girl had begun working as the second generation Lapis Lazuline. Mostly, she camped in the mountains to train, and occasionally, to see the fruits of her efforts, she would return home to help people.

I see. So that's why her home doesn't seem lived in, thought Shinobu. The reason it was so clean here was because her father was tidying the place up while his daughter was gone. His seemingly irresponsible but oddly diligent nature made sense when you looked at his daughter, who was continuing her training as she'd been taught, even after inheriting her new name.

"What about school?" Shinobu asked.

"I quit. Bein' a magical girl, I just don't have the time. Well, I do hang out with friends and stuff, but I don't go do everythin' with them as much as I did before."

"Your dad allows this?"

"Daddy trusts me."

Once in a blue moon, you ran into a father who could never confront his daughter about being irresponsible because he himself was irresponsible. *"The apple doesn't fall far from the tree" is pretty apt here*, Shinobu thought. "Not like it's any of my business, but it is worrying, you know... So why are you dressed like that if you're not in school?"

"My clothes from before I became a magical girl don't fit right no more, and goin' out in a joggin' suit seems kinda weird, so then all I've got is my old high school uniform."

"And the makeup?"

"Oh, it's usually in the fridge."

Shinobu hadn't been asking where the makeup was. She'd been asking for a concrete reason as to why she was wearing it. But she got the feeling that questioning her further would be foolish.

And why was she the one asking in the first place? Shinobu had followed her here figuring she'd be interrogated, but instead, Lapis Lazuline had served her snacks and pop and told the story of how she had gotten her name. "Um...aren't you going to talk about other stuff?"

"Other stuff?"

"Like...more serious matters."

"Serious matters..." The girl sat cross-legged, arms folded and head tilted. What was puzzling her so much?

"Aren't you curious about why I came here?" Shinobu finally just said it herself.

"Why ya came here? To hang out, right?"

"No, no, no, no, no. Why would I come to hang out at a time like this?"

"If not, then..." She suddenly tilted her head the other way and lifted her chin to look up at the sky...or not. She seemed to be eyeing the plastic grip attached to the end of the string that dangled from the florescent light. "Oh, I get it!" She clapped her hands. "Ya wanted to hammer out our plans or somethin', didn'tcha? Aw, you're totally right. We hafta talk shop. Man, I gotta do better next time!" She stuck her tongue out of the side of her mouth and rapped herself on the head.

When the girl had told Shinobu that the previous Lapis Lazuline had selected her, Shinobu had thought, *She was just chosen based on her color theme, wasn't she?* The teenager had proudly claimed that her talent had been discovered, but a magical girl named "Lapis Lazuline" had to have a blue color theme. Looks would be more important than talent or personality in that regard. So the previous Lapis Lazuline must have hit up all the blue-colored magical girls, and Blue Comet had been the only one of them to accept, or so Shinobu had figured.

Now she thought that assumption had been wrong.

It had to be because of her personality. For better or for worse, she wasn't very picky. She was surprisingly unconcerned and nonchalant about anyone that might do her harm and didn't worry about anything until it actually happened. She might never notice even if something did happen. The culprit wasn't her. Suspecting this girl would get Shinobu nowhere. There was no point. Just indulging her doubts about her was a waste. Why had she even come here? Her head was all messed up with distrust and paranoia, and now she wasn't acting logically. It was all because Melville had said that weird stuff. This was basically Melville's fault.

Shinobu snatched up her cup, guzzled down the cola in one go, and let out a huge burp. "This is basically Melville's fault."

"Ohhh, Melvy, huh? Yeah, I'm worried 'bout her."

"There's nothing to worry about, really. She seems okay." Shinobu got the impression Melville was tremendously okay. She had so much okay-ness that Shinobu wished she would share.

"What's the matter, Bell? Ya look beat. Well, guess that's no shocker. We're all workin' like dogs in the game, and you got even more to do since you're a detective and stuff in real life, huh?"

"Well, I *am* tired, but...anyway, I have to go."

"Huh? You ain't even done nothin' yet! Ya can't just go!" The girl stopped her, begging her to at least stay to see her daddy, so Shinobu was forced to wait until he came back to pay her respects.

From afar, the girl's father looked plain and respectable and not at all like his daughter, but when Shinobu spoke with him, he seemed delighted to have been able to meet his first real detective, and his fanboying convinced Shinobu that he and his daughter were clearly cut from the same cloth, after all.

Though the plan had been that Shinobu would just greet the girl's father and then go, her host took her hand after that and dragged her around town. Shinobu ended up furiously singing her heart out at karaoke, drinking an endless river of booze, singing some more, and repeating the process until she passed out.

☆ Shadow Gale

Kanoe's laptop was open on her desk, and Kanoe's cushion was lying at her feet. Kanoe's aroma diffuser was sitting on her windowsill, imbuing the room with Kanoe's scent. Atop the chair was Kanoe's balance ball, and on top of that was Kanoe herself. Since she was sitting on two things at once, her head was high off the ground. Mamori, sitting on the bed facing her to talk, was inevitably forced to look up at her.

It was irritating enough already that Kanoe had taken over more of Mamori's room, but making her look up at her simply to talk was going too far. Perhaps she was aware that Mamori was grinding her teeth, thinking *Why do I have to put up with this?* or perhaps not, but Kanoe continued with pride.

"The next area is the Evil King's castle, and it's not just the name that suggests this area is the last. We've discovered a message that says as much, too. We should be close to completion."

"You're saying that the game is almost over?" asked Mamori.

"That's right."

"Then if so, why have you been making me do all that work?"

"Just in case."

"Really? Is that it?"

"I'd never lie to you, would I?" Kanoe gave her a well-mannered smile, and the balance ball swayed. It was on top of an unstable chair, and Mamori silently prayed for her to fall, but Kanoe put her hand on the chair's armrest and regained her balance. "So things are going well on your end, Mamori?"

"If *you* say it's going well, I suppose it probably is." Before Mamori had tried it, she'd been worried about whether or not it would succeed, and when it had worked out in reality, she'd been honestly glad. But having to do it so many times had killed her initial joy and transformed it into pure woe at the misery that was her life of performing the monotonous task. It was a lot like a hen being forced to lay eggs forever and ever.

"No issues?" Kanoe asked.

"Just doing the same thing over and over and over."

"I see, I see. It's good things are going smoothly on your end. Oh, and it's all going quite well for me, too. It was my first time in a party of four, and I had my qualms about whether things would go smoothly in a mixed unit formed from three different parties, but those concerns have been dispelled entirely. I think I've managed to build such easy relationships with them, it's as if we've known one another not only since the game began, but long before."

"Good for you."

"And my concerns regarding combat were unfounded. Lapis Lazuline is more suited to fighting than I expected. She's strong and fast, of course, but she's fantastic in other ways as well. She has a firm, fine-tuned grasp on how to incorporate her magic in battle. And she moves with such skill—she doesn't just rely on her physical power as a magical girl. It's like she's had martial arts training."

"Mm-hmm, mm-hmm."

After an endless stream of talk, Kanoe suddenly pressed her lips shut and looked at Mamori. It seemed she'd finally noticed how indifferent her replies were. "Mamori, are you angry?"

Mamori didn't reply. With a thin smile, she gazed up at Kanoe. She gestured toward the door with her right hand—stiffly, like a rusted-out robot. "Miss."

"What is it?"

"The door is over that way."

"How kind of you to trouble yourself. Thank you for letting me know." Kanoe bounced down off the balance ball. Leaving her ball, cushion, laptop, and other personal effects where they were, she strode toward the door, put her right hand on the knob, and then muttered "Oh, that's right" as if she'd just remembered something. "I may have been a fool who failed to recognize the limits of her own ability."

"What?"

"I'm talking about bragging about being able to do something that I couldn't." Without another word, she left the room.

After she was gone, Mamori forgot her anger and recalled what Kanoe had said. That sort of remark would have been unthinkable for her, normally. Were things perhaps not going well in Kanoe's party? Had she not been tormenting or teasing Mamori just now, but rather venting her irritation?

Mamori stared at the door Kanoe had gone through.

MASTER SIDE #7

The only sound was the regular *click, click, click* of the turning Rubik's Cube and the hum of the active computers. The only moving things were the cube, transforming atop the girl's fingertip, and the magical girls displayed on the monitors.

"I wonder if Snow White's angry." There was no one to reply to the girl's remark. Heedless, she continued. "I thought we could be friends, though."

The door creaked. When she glanced over to the entrance, she saw the door had been ajar, and a breeze had moved it. There were no guests here, so that hard hit before must have broken it. The girl sighed and snapped her fingers. The door, which had been swinging back and forth without closing entirely, now shut.

"While I'm at it..." She snapped her fingers again. Pixelated blocks swallowed up the door, gradually becoming finer and then disappearing. Once the cubes were gone, the door had transformed from one with a knob into an automatic sliding door made of clouded glass. All the while, the girl continued turning the cube on her fingertip, as the situation on the monitors changed moment by moment.

"They'll get to the Evil King's castle soon. Well, I think they miiight be surprised. One of them is up to some weird stuff, so maybe it'd be a good idea to keep her from doing that the next time she tries. It's not like anything goes here, even if it's not teeechnically against the rules. And then there's the weather. A night with no stars and no moon, and a blue sky with just sun and no clouds aren't great for a game that sells itself on realism, especially when they never change. I just lost interest in a lot of this stuff at some point, you know? But it sounds like some of the players reeeally aren't into that. I do want to meet those sorts of expectations when I make the *New Magical Girl Raising Project*, y'know?"

The girl glanced over at the magical phone. The power was still off, and it didn't react in the slightest.

"I really should do something about that sidekick. It's a pain in the butt for a master to have to monitor the situation and do everything else themselves. Like, going on strike isn't gonna get you aaanywhere. Just do your job already."

The only thing Fal was doing was explaining the rules and other things within the game to the girls, perhaps wanting to help them out. She'd warned that if the girls got any hints or direct answers, she'd delete the whole game, players and all, so Fal wasn't going to defy her. But despite the order not to tell them directly, the mascot could still provide leads that a sharp magical girl could pick up on, like that time with the event where the one with the fewest candy would lose. Fal had deliberately emphasized that "the player who holds the smallest amount of candy will die."

Well, it's fine if that's all it is, I guess, the girl thought. She wasn't about to challenge Fal over it. "Don't tell them directly" meant that indirect means were not disallowed. So she would keep to what she'd said.

"Just read them the lines I've ordered you to read, though. No additions. If there's any funny business, I'm deleting the whole game." She'd give Fal a warning, at least. There was no reply, but the sidekick had to have heard her.

If Fal was going to be giving out clues, then it was a good thing she'd kept the truth about the Evil King to herself. If they got any hints about the Evil King, even in an indirect way, everything would be spoiled. The girl hated the Evil King, but even so, she'd gone to a lot of trouble to make this game.

Keeping secrets from her helper, to whom she would normally have to tell everything, did make this game more game-like, though. The fact that only the master knew about the Evil King was what made this into a *real* game. She wanted to take advantage of that the next time, too.

The girl pulled her finger away from the Rubik's Cube. Even with its support gone, the cube kept clicking and shifting in midair.

CHAPTER 8
NOTHING LEFT ANYMORE

☆ **Nokko**

Though it had been explained to her beforehand, Nokko was startled when she logged into the game and found herself suddenly in the library area with Pfle, Detec Bell, and Lapis Lazuline nearby. When Nokko was surprised, she wouldn't be the only one feeling it, since she transmitted her emotions around her, so she calmed herself down as best she could and looked around. The full party was there, and Detec Bell and Lapis Lazuline yelped in shock as they looked around.

The Initial Location Switch Device that Pfle had acquired through *R* was a convenient item. It could change where a party would appear when they logged into the game. No matter how fast magical girls were, going all the way from the wasteland to their desired area was still a lot of wasted effort. Though new gates between the regions appeared in various places once an area was unlocked, like from the wasteland to the mountains or from the

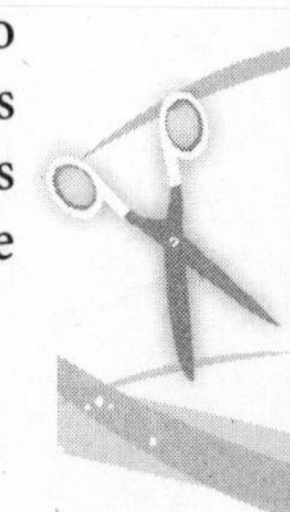

mountains to the library—they'd learned where these were from the map application—it still took time to get around.

There was one more reason that Nokko was glad to have the Initial Location Switch Device. Nobody said it aloud, but this was the more important reason.

It was because of how Masked Wonder had been murdered and her items stolen. The killer had done it in the period between when they logged in and when she would have met up with her party. They'd gotten her while she was alone. With this device, that interval would vanish for them. The whole party would be together from the moment they logged in.

The vague understanding that the culprit had been @Meow-Meow had proliferated among all the girls. In Nokko's opinion, this was because Genopsyko had hinted that there was a traitor. Since she had already suggested that it might be the case, they believed she had sacrificed her life to tell them who it was. Nokko, who had been with @Meow-Meow and Genopsyko, didn't think that was true, but if asked, *So what do you think?* she would stall and say she didn't really know.

Nokko didn't think @Meow-Meow was the culprit, but her opinion wasn't going to convince anyone, and she wasn't going to try to convince them. But she was certain there was still someone among them who meant harm, and she wanted to be as alert as possible for that. Nokko wasn't a powerful fighter, so she had to rely on others to be alert for her as well. This meant that it was best for her to stick with her party as much as possible. If Nokko were some fantastically powerful magical girl, the game might have already ended by now. But that was just an escapist fantasy, so Nokko decided to focus on grappling with reality.

The proliferation of the theory that the traitor was @Meow-Meow also supported an idea that had been suggested earlier, that all the parties cooperate. The elimination of the suspicious individuals had eased their anxieties about talking to someone whose loyalties were unknown. Now that the end of the game was in sight, the two parties had the chance to cooperate whenever it was even slightly useful for completion. They were bringing each other hints, helping out when more numbers were needed, and attempting to share knowledge of the monsters as much as possible.

In the course of their monster-killing, the others brought the items Nokko's party had requested—Clantail speaking little, Nonako Miyokata and Rionetta quarreling, and Pechka...being timid. She was always nervous and flustered. *I'm surprised she was able to become a magical girl, if that's how she is,* thought Nokko.

Though it was technically "cooperation between all parties," there were only two, so if both of them were of a mind to cooperate, that would end up happening. Even Melville, who was apparently off somewhere exploring alone, would pop up from wherever she had been to help them some, bearing hint messages she'd found or information regarding places that seemed to be quest-related.

And speaking of soloists, Shadow Gale was most likely by herself, too, but Nokko had no idea what she was doing and where right about then. Their party never encountered her, even though they explored every corner of the library area. She might have been somewhere else, but what would she be doing outside the library at this point? When Nokko had asked Pfle, she'd simply shrugged in a sort of blunt refusal, saying, "I suppose she's just doing whatever she wants."

Between the strength and nature of the monsters and the ability to avoid battles by sitting in a chair, the library area was, as the word "library" might imply, not as combat-focused as the subterranean area had been. This was also apparent in the quest to unlock the Evil King's castle. Compared to the quest to defeat the Great Dragon, it required more brains—or rather, more persistence.

"I'd love to get some hints on the correct order here," said Detec Bell.

"'Squares into a circle,' huh?" Pfle muttered.

"A bunch of the titles are the same, too."

"The covers and pages are all the same. Only the titles differ. But you're saying some titles are identical."

Pfle and Detec Bell were discussing the order of the books. It was basically a code, so Nokko went around the library in search of books so as not to bother the pair. Not only was Lazuline a good fighter, but also her intuition was sharp. Even when monsters would catch them in a pincer attack from before and behind, she could deftly manage their attacks without even glancing over her shoulder. When Nokko was exploring with her, they never got caught by surprise, which was really reassuring.

"All thanks to my master's trainin'," Lazuline had said. Nokko was thankful to this master, who was now retired from being a magical girl, according to Lazuline.

There was an empty bookshelf on the eastern end of the library—without even a single book. What's more, while most books in the library had only white pages, a few featured pages of such a deep red, Nokko suspected that if she ran her finger down one, it would dye her fingertip.

According to the hints in the library, collecting these books and setting them into the empty bookshelf in a specific order would open the gate to the next area. But though it had been hinted that there was a specific order, there were no instructions on what that was. They had to figure that part out on their own. Their only other hint was the phrase *squares into a circle*.

Pfle and Detec Bell's heated discussion was about the order of the books. Nokko thought they should at least gather all the books before they started talking about that, but once they'd gathered about 90 percent, the pair had leaned in close to each other and started in: "No, it's not this," and "No, it's not that."

☆ Detec Bell

The moment before Shinobu Hioka had gone from the real world into the game again, she'd been unconscious. She remembered being in the karaoke booth drinking, and then finally belting out some songs, but her memories ended there. When she came to, she was transformed into Detec Bell, sitting on a chair in the library area. After about a minute of confusion, she found out this was the effect of the Initial Location Switch Device that Pfle had acquired through *R*.

Because *R* was so unreliable, it hadn't really been a part of the strategy for Detec Bell's party, but the device was convenient. Cutting their travel time short put her at ease. *Maybe it's not such a bad idea to give* R *a shot if we've got the spare candy*, she thought. But the game would probably be over before they had any to spare. *Magical Girl Raising Project* was finally reaching its climax.

With the help of Clantail's party, and Melville, too, they collected enough of the red books to fill the empty bookshelf. They invited Clantail to help them figure out what order the books had to go in, but she had replied that they would leave the puzzle-solving to Pfle's party, and in the meantime, their party would go kill some monsters to stock up candy. Melville gave them the same answer, so Detec Bell figured that perhaps their interest in this subject simply differed.

While she was discussing with Pfle, Detec Bell tried putting the books on the shelf a number of times and failed. The bookshelf wouldn't accept books in the wrong order. It would make a beeping sound and spit them all out again. Then she would pick them all up and consider the matter again from a different angle.

Detec Bell tried holding the books over a flame. She tried sniffing them. She tried dripping water on them. Then Pfle informed her that she'd already tried all those things, so Detec Bell gave up on that. She flipped through the pages and racked her brains, wondering if there was some kind of pattern. Even using her magnifying glass, she couldn't find anything.

Squares into a circle. Squares into a circle. Squares into a circle…

"Bell, Bell!"

While lost in thought, Detec Bell suddenly heard someone speaking to her. She looked up and saw Lazuline grinning at her.

"What?" she asked.

"I think bein' a detective's a good idea."

"…For who?"

"For me."

"Why?"

"I always thought ya were this cool, clever detective, but I had no idea ya had all that passion bottled up inside! After I heard that super-enthusiastic speech, I just had to be a detective myself! And well, I've been thinkin' lately that I can't always have my daddy be payin' for an unemployed magical girl. I'll use all the skills my master taught me to work to become the Legendary Detective: Lapis Lazuline!"

"Oh…okay." Now Detec Bell knew what she'd been babbling about and to whom while she'd been drinking. But now that she knew, she really didn't want to be hearing about it at the moment. She didn't want Lazuline to blab about anything else, and not just because the other magical girls would hear. She didn't want Lazuline going on about Detec Bell's drunken nonsense as if it were praiseworthy. "All right, then as your first step on the path to being a detective, come help me investigate."

"Roger!"

Detec Bell had come to understand something from being in a party with Pfle: Detec Bell was not very good at solving puzzles. Back in the real world, she could use her magic and physical strength to solve mysteries, but the moment she had come into the game and had her magic restricted, she'd come to a halt. Pfle was abnormally sharp. Detec Bell couldn't even feel jealous. She seemed very much like the famous detectives Shinobu had admired.

She ended up thinking, *Well, maybe some detectives just aren't as good at deduction.* It was a little funny that she could consider the idea and be so calm about it. Now she couldn't understand why she had been so upset back when Melville had left. Had she changed because they were close to their goal, or because Lazuline had recognized her? For better or for worse, Lazuline's carefree antics made Detec Bell less anxious. Why had she been so paranoid before? It was all so baffling.

For her own part, Lazuline was humming as she fought monsters. Detec Bell couldn't be like that, nor did she want to.

Detec Bell thoroughly searched the library area and came back with the last hint: *First comes now.*

"'Now,' hmm?" Pfle took a book in one hand. It was a book titled precisely that: *Now.* "So, beginning with the book titled *Now*...make the squares into a circle, *hmm*...?" Pfle muttered as she began setting books on the bookshelf. The title *Now* was three letters long. The next book in line had a title that was fourteen letters long. Next, she looked for a book that had fifteen letters, and after that, nine, and then she searched for a long title with twenty-six letters, then five, and then three.

3.1415926535897932...squares into a circle. That is to say, use the square books to make pi.

Pfle had figured out that you had to line up the books in the shelf by the number of letters in their titles to create pi, and they opened the gate to the Evil King's castle.

☆ Shadow Gale

Each new area of the game had different smells. The wasteland area smelled like earth, the grasslands area smelled like air, and here, the odor of mold hung over everything.

Perhaps because it was a game, the smells wouldn't follow you if you left an area. It wouldn't get into your clothes or on your skin, either. That was an honest relief to Shadow Gale. She could put up with the earth and the grass, but mold had to be near the top on the list of smells she couldn't stand. It would have been absolutely miserable if it had stuck to her clothes and skin and never come out. A magical girl should smell like flowers and fruit. If she had to appear with a whiff of mold, she'd be a joke.

The moldy smell hanging all around her, Shadow Gale set the Dragon-Killer in her firing device and pointed it toward the Great Dragon. The dragon threatened her with a deafening roar that shook the entire cavern. The first time she'd heard that sound, she'd shuddered from the depths of her soul, but by now, she'd heard it so many times that it just seemed repetitive and didn't bother her.

She pressed the switch on the firing device, and the Dragon-Killer shot off. She got a perfect hit on the Great Dragon, and the earth trembled as it fell. This felt pedestrian to her, too. The first time, she'd trembled with joy at having defeated the Great Dragon all by herself, but that emotion had quickly evaporated, too. She didn't even remember how many times she'd done this already.

By defeating the Great Dragon, she won the Dragon Shield. Now she didn't even have to look at her magical phone. She knew the item was there.

Cautiously avoiding all the various traps set on the floor here, Shadow Gale left the cavern. Pfle had told her that as long as there was a player-killer out there, she should be extremely cautious when on her own, so Shadow Gale had set up a trap within the Great Dragon's cavern. The trap would also fire mercilessly on anyone who stepped in innocently, but according to Pfle, if that happened, they were "just unlucky."

But at this point in time, the library was the newest area, and everyone would be exploring and killing monsters over there. Shadow Gale would be the only one secluding herself down here, defeating the Great Dragon over and over.

She sighed. Midgame bosses generally didn't respawn. But selling off the special item the Great Dragon dropped made the event recur and revived it. Pfle had been the one to discover this fact.

So Shadow Gale had to take the shield to the shop and sell it off. Once she'd sold it, she'd confront the Great Dragon once more. She could see no end to this loop.

☆ Pechka

A mysterious, sweet scent floated in the air, though it wasn't the only thing here. The sparkling marble floors were starkly different from the old wooden floorboards of the library area. There was not a single scratch on the ground, and the tapping of hooves on it sounded pleasant. Though they were indoors, there was no risk of Clantail kicking through the floor, and she could freely transform into large animals.

Rionetta scowled and pressed her skirts in. "This floor is so sorely over-polished, it even reflects the underside of my skirts."

"Yeah, and everyone wants to see a doll's bloomers, *hein*?"

"If you must say such vulgar things, then please do it when I'm not present."

Rionetta and Nonako were at it, as usual. They never changed, even now, in the final area. It seemed like they were deliberately sniping at each other, even, keeping everything the same. Their fights seemed a bit more forced than usual. Or maybe it just looked that way to Pechka because she was anxious.

The final area: the Evil King's castle.

It was a splendid, marble-wrought palace. The hallways, big enough for five Pechkas to lie next to each other spread-eagle, were decorated at intervals with sculptures, large statues, and great paintings in magnificent frames. But because of the "Evil King" part of the castle's name, all the art had some twisted element to it: batlike wings growing from the back of a beautiful woman, or two curving goat-horns on the temples of a bearded gentleman.

After they had passed through the gate from the library area, they had immediately emerged into a hallway. The gate behind them was at a dead end, and the hallway extended before them about a hundred yards before it turned to the right.

"Everyone, good luck. Don't let your guard down," said Pfle, sitting on her magic carpet at their center. The assembled magical girls all nodded. The members of Pechka's party weren't the only ones there. Detec Bell's group was there, too, along with Pfle, Shadow Gale, and Melville—who Pechka hadn't seen in a while—and Nokko, too. Shadow Gale was eyeing Pfle a little resentfully. Something had probably happened between the two of them.

When they encountered monsters, they'd check the monster encyclopedia first.

They weren't about to go immediately charging in simply because they'd discovered the Evil King's location.

Going off on your own was strictly forbidden.

No rushing, no impatience.

Counting on her fingers, Pechka double-checked that everyone was there. It was looking like there'd be no particular issues if they proceeded as usual.

"Now then, let's go," said Pfle.

None of them were fixated on parties anymore. With the formerly solo Melville and Shadow Gale added to the group, they promised solidarity to each other.

In the lead were Clantail, Lapis Lazuline, and Rionetta. The second line consisted of Melville, Nokko, and Detec Bell. The third line consisted of Pechka and Pfle on her magic carpet. At the rear were Nonako Miyokata and Shadow Gale. Fortunately, the ceiling was over thirty feet high, so they positioned Nonako's dragon in the air as a support/confusion tactic/scout for when the time came. Plus, it could also watch out for attacks from above.

This arrangement had most likely been decided based on their abilities, roles in combat or whatnot. But to Pechka, being separated from the allies she knew and positioned among magical girls she didn't know very well was anxiety- and stress-inducing. She was beginning to timidly walk forward when she received a poke in the rear. Her heart leaped into her mouth.

"Relax, *s'il vous plaît*! I said I'd protect you, Pechka," said Nonako Miyokata.

"Oh...of course. Um...thank you...very much." Pechka was grateful and glad, and she felt she could rely on Nonako. But she would rather hear it in a way that didn't give her a heart attack.

"Oh! Stop, stop!" A loud voice came from up front, and Pechka's heart jumped again. "There's somethin' on the ground. It's set to spring somethin' on ya if ya step on it." What Lazuline was pointing at looked just like a completely normal spot on the marble floor. "Man, it's the final level, so there's gonna be traps and stuff, y'know? I was zonin' out since we ain't seen nothin' like that so far. I just found it at the last minute. That was real close, seriously."

They all murmured anxiously. "Can you see anything?" "Yeah." "Oh, you're right—there's signs it's been tampered with." "I can't tell..." "But she says something *est là*." "Wot a caereless mistaeke." "Hmm..."

Some of the girls couldn't tell at all, some at least noticed something was off, some could notice if they looked closely, and others could tell clearly even from a distance... Well, only Lazuline could do that. But apparently, there was some variation in what they saw.

Pfle clapped her hands. Everyone shut their mouths and turned their attention to her. "There's no question that something is there?" she asked Lazuline.

"I mean, can't ya tell just by lookin'?" The issue here was that some of them couldn't, but Lazuline was operating on the assumption that they were all on the same page. They weren't.

"I'd like to avoid any problem spots as we move along... It's highly likely someone might inadvertently step on one of these."

"So then should I mark it?" Lazuline suggested.

"That would be all right if what the trap senses is weight or body heat, but if vibration is the trigger, and it activates the moment it's touched, it'll be no laughing matter."

"I've an idea." Rionetta raised her hand. The way her ball joints bent was humanlike, extending elegantly to the tips of her fingers.

The sound of marble striking marble was obnoxiously loud and grating to the ears. The weight of the stone statue had to be measured in tons, and the vibrations reached all the way to Pechka over a hundred and fifty feet away. The large golem's feet slowly thundered down the hallway of the Evil King's castle.

"Right around there, is that correct?" asked Rionetta.

"Yeah, a little to the right...there, there, right there," replied Lazuline.

The muscular marble statue, wearing only a loincloth to cover the necessary areas, dropped its foot on the part of the floor Lazuline indicated. As the powerful blast roared, purple flashes burned on the girls' retinas.

"It seems that was a lightning trap," said Pfle.

The marble all around was soot-black. The muscular statue that had stepped on the trap was covered all over in soot, too, but it still lifted its foot with a creak from the spot where the trap had been. Somehow, it could still keep walking.

"Hooold on just a sec, guys!" Lazuline trotted up to the center of the explosion site and then gave a wave. "The trap's gone! Looks like once you step on it once, it's done!"

"Fantastic," said Pfle. "Well then, let's proceed with this plan: We'll have the statues scout for us and step on traps for us. That will be safest."

A high-pitched laugh sounded out. Rionetta's right hand was against her mouth as she laughed haughtily. "It seems that *finally* I can put my specialty to good use. I hadn't seen a single doll thus far, so I worried that I might perhaps spend this whole game as just another fighter."

"So a statue counts as a doll to you?" Nonako Miyokata remarked. "Your magic is unreasonably flexible, *hein*?"

"I shan't accept such accusations from someone who treats everything from goblins to dragons as beasts."

They had three marble statues in total: one with a black goat head, a human torso, and a goat's lower body; a beautiful woman with large bat's wings growing from her back; and the macho statue that had just crushed the trap. Rionetta said that a doll's speed and ability to take a hit depended on what it was made of, and that the marble statues were slow to move and solidly built.

The statues would not be suited to fighting faster monsters but would be optimal for stepping on traps, Rionetta had proudly declared. Pechka also understood quite well how good it felt when your apparently useless magic had its moment of glory.

Since now they knew there were traps, their formation had been adjusted slightly. The three marble statues stomped along heavily over a hundred and fifty feet ahead of the group. "I could control quite a few more, but too many would become a hindrance, I daresay?" Rionetta commented.

Lapis Lazuline joined the statues as their scout, since she had been the first one to discover that trap. There had been some concern as to what Lazuline would do if they ran into monsters and she became the focus of their attacks, but she had said, "I'll just hand one of these to Taily in the front. With my super teleportation powers, I can pop right over to her if something happens up there, so I'll be okay."

Lazuline's magic was instant teleportation to her lapis lazuli. She could teleport anywhere as long as there was a gem there. If Lazuline handed one of her gems to someone in the rear guard, she could join them immediately.

Detec Bell gave Lazuline strict orders to come straight back to them if any monsters appeared, no matter how weak they looked, and Lazuline was deployed with the vanguard to scout for enemies and traps. And so they made their way forward, checking for threats as they went. Slowly and steadily, inch by inch, they proceeded down the hall. Occasionally, they discovered a trap, and each time, Lazuline and two of the three statues would retreat while the remaining statue set it off. There was a lightning trap, flammable gas with an ignition device, lines of spears, explosions, and a trap that looked like a like mysterious, glowing magic sigil. They couldn't tell at a glance what that one did. Going through a number of the traps destroyed the statues, so Rionetta activated new ones from among the statues decorating the hall and incorporated them into their formation.

The hallway was long. It didn't just seem that way because they were forced to advance so slowly. There were actually no rooms and no doors aside from the gates they'd first walked in through.

"I see," Pfle muttered as she turned on her magical phone and examined the screen. Taking a peek from the side, Pechka could see she had launched the map application that showed them their surroundings. "It seems we're going clockwise toward a center."

The screen displayed a spiral-like shape. It went forward, then turned right, forward, right, forward, right, over and over. *Now that she mentions it—she's right. We've never gone left*, thought Pechka. So far, they'd turned right twice, so that meant they were still circling the outer perimeter. The magical phone also displayed the current locations of their party members.

"Stop!" Lazuline called out from the front, and everyone stopped. About fifty yards ahead of the vanguard and a hundred ahead of Pechka and the rest, light was streaming in from one side of the hall.

Pfle checked the map displayed on her magical phone. "There's an opening, about fifteen feet wide, that leads to a space of about thirty square feet. It doesn't look to be connected to anything beyond. It may be a terrace of some sort."

Lazuline walked briskly, craning her neck to peer at the opening that was letting the light through. Detec Bell's fists were clenched and trembling as she muttered, "How can she act so unguarded?"

Lazuline, oblivious to Detec Bell's internal anxieties, slipped nimbly into the light. This time, she poked just her head back out of it, then turned toward them. "Found the shop!"

"Ooh!" someone exclaimed. The girls all quickened their pace a little to join Lazuline, breaking off into groups to visit the shop and check out the goods.

Just as Pfle had predicted, it was a balcony that let in light and air from the outside. Its railing was finely ornamented with the same sort of devilish creatures featured in the paintings and carvings adorning the castle halls. On the middle of the railing sat a bisque urn about half as big as Pechka herself. When they activated their magical phones there, the displays indicated that the urn was the shop. Apparently, transactions were carried out by putting things into and taking things out of the urn.

Some of the girls wanted to discuss the shop's items, while others were hungry and looking to eat something, and since these two suggestions didn't conflict, they decided to take a break for a meal in front of the shop. Since there were now more than twice as many people as had been in her party before, Pechka was that much busier. She packed the debris from the broken marble statues into a pot and made congee with lots of vegetables and meat.

The smell of Pechka's cooking wafted into the air, overwhelming the characteristic sweet scent of this area. The aroma of the dish sped up and slowed down, drafting around the group, with the motion from everyone's spoons. This smell was far more calming. Pechka breathed a sigh.

"This is *so* good!" crowed Lapis Lazuline. "Crazy good! Y'all were keepin' the good stuff to yourselves! It's a crime!"

"So says the girl from the party that kept the hunting grounds to themselves. The *gall*," Rionetta quipped.

"That's different! Man, this is so damn good!"

"You don't have to scarf it down so fast. No one's going to steal it from you." Detec Bell admonished Lazuline for her bad manners as the girl in blue intently gobbled down her food. Meanwhile, beside her, Detec Bell herself was eating as if her life depended on it.

Pfle's demeanor belied the amount she was packing into her stomach as she commented on the seasoning, cooking method, and ingredients. Shadow Gale was still eyeing Pfle resentfully, but even so, she seemed to be enjoying the food. Pechka didn't really understand what Melville was saying, and Lazuline wasn't translating since she was concentrating on eating instead. But from Melville's expression and reactions, Pechka figured she was probably being complimentary. Nokko helped serve everyone. As a maid, she was used to it.

Clantail's tail was wagging widely, and for some reason, Nonako was proudly bragging about the food. Pechka didn't let it show much, but in fact she was even prouder than Nonako that they all enjoyed her cooking. Pechka was bad at fighting, average at exploring, couldn't solve puzzles, and didn't have any other useful skills or magic. Cooking was the only thing she could do to make everyone happy, and it made her glad.

The smell of the food stuck to them, even after the meal was done. The congee's aroma wafted on ahead, drowning out the sickly sweetness of the Evil King's castle. Pechka prayed that it would last forever.

☆ Shadow Gale

The shop in the Evil King's castle, the final area, was the final shop of the game, in other words. Of course the goods were powerful, expensive, and their circulation limit numbers were low.

There was a weapon +10 and a Shield +10. Both were insanely expensive. What's more, they were limited to just one each.

"Only one of each item is for sale," commented Pfle, "and they're expensive, to boot. We wouldn't be able to buy these even if we defeated a hundred fiends. The master predicted we'd all be scrambling to get at these first...assuming we weren't united, that is." But now they had settled on the goal of attempting to defeat the Evil King as a unified group. They just had to pool all their candy to buy the items, then give them to the players who seemed like they'd be most effective with them. "Their plan may have been for the players to fight among themselves over the limited number of powerful weapons. This means that in unifying, we've surpassed the master's expectations." Only the smug-faced Pfle knew how seriously she meant that.

They decided to give the weapon +10 to Melville and have Clantail use the Shield +10. Of course, receiving powerful weapons was not entirely cause for excitement. In accepting this powerful weapon and shield, these girls were essentially being told that they'd be fighting at the front of the pack when the time came. *I'll just do my best not to get in the way*, Shadow Gale was thinking, when Pfle said, "Oh, Mamori. You have the Dragon Shield, the strongest of them all, so be sure to fight the hardest. I've entrusted you a very important position at the rear because I have great expectations for you in combat."

"...Can I trade with someone else?" Shadow Gale asked.

"You've been using it longest, so you must be used to it."

Shadow Gale wanted to slap Pfle's face for making such a remark so nonchalantly. Would she at least be allowed to flick her on the forehead?

The other items included a "stun gun"—this late in the game, for some reason.

The stun gun on sale at this shop was a "stun baton" type, and it was used by touching it to your opponent and pushing a button on the handle with your thumb to send an electric current running through it. The encyclopedia said its effect on enemies of the "evil" class was instantaneous, knocking out any evil-type enemy immediately and keeping them out for thirty minutes.

Then there was the even more confusing "flamethrower."

The flamethrower, successfully shrunk to machine-gun size, was small enough that it was easy to handle and swing around, even for a small-statured magical girl. Just like the stun gun, it was very effective on evil-type enemies, and three sprays of flame would burn the enemy black.

Shadow Gale purchased a flamethrower to test it out, pointing it at the sky off the terrace and pulling the trigger. It spewed a massive flame about six feet in diameter, and the heat and size of the flames made her wince and yelp.

"By 'evil-type,' do they mean the fiends and wraiths?"

"Those are demon-type, apparently."

"That's so confusing…"

"There are no evil-type monsters in the monster encyclopedia. Most likely, right here…" Pfle pointed to the *???* spots in the monster encyclopedia. There were only two types of enemies left that were listed as question marks—in other words, two that they hadn't encountered yet. "…is where the evil-type monsters go."

Two types left, and one of them, at least, would be the Evil King. The other would be a secondary boss before the Evil King or random encounters that would show up on their way there. Of course, even if they were the latter, that didn't mean they were trash mobs. Often, large numbers proved far more daunting than a weaker boss.

"I wouldn't even be able to laugh if we beat the Evil King with a stun gun or a flamethrower," said Shadow Gale.

"It would be a fitting end to this ridiculous mess."

They took turns on watch until the meal was over, set up their formation again, and resumed their advance. Shadow Gale was marching after them all at the tail. The sight of the whole crowd going forward, shields up (aside from Melville, who couldn't equip a shield due to the nature of her weapon) reminded her of a bomb squad she'd once seen on TV.

Nonako Miyokata, who was at the rear with Shadow Gale, poked Pechka in front of her to talk to her. Every poke startled Pechka, making her jump, and Shadow Gale had to feel sorry for her. And since Nonako didn't seem at all like she was paying attention to their surroundings, that meant as they walked, Shadow Gale had to be on guard for attacks or followers from behind. It was exhausting. But still, she cheered herself up by telling herself she had a better deal than Lazuline and the three up front doing the hard work of searching for traps as they advanced.

Their progress was slow. They would occasionally set off traps, then turn right and go forward again, over and over. Since the hallway went in an inward-turning spiral, the farther they got, the shorter the straightaways became. Shadow Gale turned on her magical phone and activated the map application to check how far they'd come. One player icon was displayed about two-thirds of the way down the route. *We've gotten pretty far*, she thought, but at the same time, she recalled that she was the only member of her party, so she didn't feel much better.

From that point onward, they continued to prioritize safety as they advanced, intermittently breaking for meals and dealing with over a hundred traps until the whole party arrived at their goal point.

While everything around them—walls, ceiling, and furnishings—was white marble, what blocked their way at the end of the hallway was a wooden door. They didn't have to speculate about what lay beyond it. Someone blew out a breath. Shadow exhaled a deep sigh as well. The game was about to end. The road had been long. It had been only around two weeks, but it had felt so, so long. Six people had died to get them this far.

Lazuline, who had been checking the door, raised both her arms to make a circle. "No traps."

"Is it locked?" asked Pfle.

"Nope. I figure pushin' it should open it up."

"Then please do."

Lazuline gently pushed the door, and it opened inward with a creak. When they peeked inside, it seemed to be a room. What looked like an armor-clad knight and plastic robot stood side by side. They seemed like decorations—but then they started moving, and the magical girls raised their weapons and shields.

☆ **Nokko**

The knight had horns like a dragon and a large, reptilian tail…and if the tail was anything like the horns, it was probably a dragon's, too. Nokko was startled, recalling @Meow-Meow, but the knight strode toward them, heedless of her reaction. A helmet and face guard covered its head, casting its visage in shadow, so she couldn't really see it. Swiftly, the knight pulled a massive two-handed sword from the scabbard on its back.

The robot was floating in the air. There was something like a backpack strapped to its back, spurting flame. Its red eyes were plastic, just like its body, and its whole form made it clear that it had been created by people. In midair, it spread all four limbs out, and small objects flew out of its backpack toward them, trailing white smoke.

—Missiles?!

Nokko held her shield at a diagonal, dropping her right knee to the marble floor to prepare for the impact. She felt the thunderous shaking of the explosion as thick white smoke billowed up. It looked like someone else had blocked it. Then something sliced through the white smoke above. When Nokko raised her head, the robot had paused in the air, splayed out again. Nokko was about to turn her shield around to face the new direction when she heard a cry from behind her. Following that came the sound of metal hitting metal.

"It's an Evil King's Knight and a Hell Jester! Nonelemental! No weaknesses or strengths!" Pfle, in the middle of checking the monster encyclopedia, took a hit and was slammed into Nokko's back.

Shield still up, Nokko rolled forward, then somehow regained her balance with her shield facing above her when heat and another shock hit her and launched her backward into a wall. Pfle was grimacing, but she continued to cling to her magic carpet, refusing to let go and just barely staying in place. She wasn't looking at the monster encyclopedia anymore; it had been knocked to the ground. She yelled, "No weaknesses or strengths! Just hammer them down!"

Through the billowing white smoke, Nokko could see a faint black shadow fifteen feet ahead. It was raising something up. Nokko braced her shield and blocked the attack, but her arm felt numb. After blocking a second and then third attack, her arm couldn't handle any more, and she dropped the shield. It hit the floor with a clang, and she abandoned it there and darted to the side. The knight's sword left a violent gash in the marble floor, a visceral reminder of the knight's physical prowess and sharp blade.

Gradually, the white smoke cleared. Rising to her knees, Nokko looked around in horror. Lazuline and was trading blows with a knight; Melville was targeting the robot flying above them with her javelins; Nonako and her dragon had trapped another knight between them in a pincer attack; Rionetta and Clantail were defending Pechka from three more knights; Detec Bell and Shadow Gale were being pushed farther and further back, unable to even attack; and Pfle huddled on her magic carpet, shield still up, continuously blocking a stream of attacks and unable to escape. There were as many enemies as there were magical girls.

Each and every one of them was stronger than any monster so far, aside from the Great Dragon. The knights' swords were unusually powerful and heavy, and Nokko couldn't even block their strikes entirely. Her arm was still tingling, and she couldn't get it to move right.

Now that Nokko was without her shield, the enemy swung at her again. She jumped back to avoid the blow...but couldn't dodge it entirely. She hadn't escaped the knight's range. Its sword was massive and long. Nokko swung her mop, throwing her entire body into a strike against the flat of the knight's blade to forcefully change its trajectory. But the power behind the knight's swing knocked her down, and she banged her shoulder against the wall. She couldn't dodge the next swing, so she blocked it with her mop in place of the shield. The lone hit bent her weapon +7 mop, which she'd paid a high price for in candy.

Someone screamed—Pechka. Nokko wanted to plug her ears. Screaming was not what she wanted to hear right now. She mustered an aggressive desire to destroy their enemies to take over her heart. She filled herself with the kind of fighting spirit that would make you put your life on the line for the sake of your allies, to fight heroically, and spread it to the others around her. If any of the girls had the time to scream, she should be taking down one more enemy instead. She transmitted these feelings to all around her.

Nokko stood up, smacking the knight's sword hilt hard with her bent mop to lock weapons with her enemy, but the knight easily knocked her back again. It was so much stronger. *I'm not going to let this beat me*, she thought, and she struck it again with her mop as she launched her indomitable spirit around her.

Pechka raised her shield and joined the front lines, which lessened the strain on Rionetta and Clantail, who had been forced to protect her. Clantail pulled out her magical phone and switched it on. Countless spears had been thrust into the floor around her. Clantail transformed her body into a great octopus, grabbed a spear in each tentacle, and assaulted the knights. At this point, it was hard to tell who was the monster.

Nokko kept on praying. *Fight, fight, fight, fight.*

Melville focused on fixing her aim, ignoring the missile coming at her. The blast hit her as she flung her javelin to destroy the robot's booster. The robot lost its balance, went into a tailspin, and plunged into the floor. Blood streaming from her head, Melville chucked another javelin to destroy the robot's head entirely. But though that should have finished it off, it raised itself up again. *What?* thought Nokko, but the robot immediately grabbed at one of the knights fighting nearby. This confused Nokko for a moment until she figured out that Rionetta had to be controlling it.

Lazuline slammed a knight into the wall with a roundhouse kick, then rushed in for a flurry of punches from both hands, hammering the thick metal armor out of shape.

Waiting until the moment a knight raised its sword, Pfle leaped at it from her magic carpet, wrapped her arms around the knight's neck, and wrenched it upside down.

Unable to withstand the coordinated assault from Nonako and her dragon, another knight dropped its sword and fell to its knees, and Detec Bell and Shadow Gale were somehow managing to hold their own, too.

With things like this, one of them would surely come in soon to help Nokko. Brandishing her mop, Nokko was relieved.

Defeated, the knights fell to the ground in pieces of armor. The robot remained as a lump of plastic and iron, away from them in a corner of the hallway. In two hours, it would vanish.

Nonako was indignant. "I can't believe they didn't give us any living *créatures*!"

"Now then. Are we ready?" said Pfle.

They had healed up. The recovery medicine had cured all of them, both the girls with serious injuries and the ones who'd received milder wounds. Those like Nokko, whose weapons had broken, borrowed from those who had extra. All of them were 100 percent prepared, weapons and shields at the ready. They heard the tense hum of Melville pulling her bowstring taut.

The room the knights and robot had occupied was perfectly square, about thirty square feet in area, and there was a door on the other end that led onward. It was a size smaller than the way they'd come in, but garishly decorated. It was metal, engraved with faces in various states of agony. Its black shone in contrast with the white of the marble. It was sickening, pompous, and sinister.

Nokko looked at the map application on her phone. The room beyond this door was the end of the Evil King's castle. That meant once they opened this door, they'd have reached their goal.

Lazuline, done investigating the gate, made a circle with her arms. "No traps, and it's not locked! It opens like normal!"

"Good," said Pfle. "Then everyone, to your positions."

Their strongest fighters were at the front, those who weren't as good came next, and those who were, frankly speaking, more of a drag, came after that. Melville, who could attack from a distance, followed at the rear.

"We're prepared. You're all powerful. But still, as long as the Evil King's strength is an unknown, our powers may not be enough. If it seems victory is impossible, run as fast as you can. As long as we all survive, there will be a way." Pfle shot Clantail a look, signaling her to slowly, carefully open the door.

The room was completely undecorated on the inside, featuring only a single chair inside the pure-white marble space. It was magnificent, the sort that a king would sit on in a game, in manga, or some other story. It was worthy of being called a throne. Nokko glanced at Pechka beside her. Pechka looked like she didn't understand what she was seeing.

Cautiously, Clantail and Lazuline entered, and the other magical girls followed. Even once they were inside, nothing happened, and the girls gradually became bolder and willing to explore more freely. Still, nothing. The room was silent except for the noises the girls made themselves as they milled about.

"Hold on. There's something written on the back of the chair." There were markings like text carved into the marble backrest. Pfle activated Translator Buddy to translate the writing into Japanese. The display on the app said, The Evil King is absent and is currently being chased around by fifteen magical girls. Please come again.

"...What?" Pfle touched the throne with her hand, and then her magical phone sounded with an alert, signaling the arrival of an announcement.

A player has reached the Evil King's throne and fulfilled the condition for memory unlock. The Evil King's crisis will raise the monsters' morale. The monsters' level will now rise.

On a basic level, the message had to mean that the monsters

had gotten stronger, but Nokko didn't understand what was going on or why.

"Where...is the Evil King?" Clantail muttered.

None of them could give her an answer.

☆ **Pechka**

They investigated every inch of the throne room and still couldn't find a thing. They searched the castle but uncovered no messages or hints—and of course, neither did they encounter the Evil King.

They were all confused and angry. It was as if the ladder they were climbing had suddenly been moved. Right when they'd been thinking they had nearly reached their objective, that they could finish this game, the goalposts had vanished.

Pfle used her magical phone to summon Fal. Even before she started asking questions, Fal was agitated and bouncing side to side, scattering gold powder. "The Evil King must exist, pon. Absolutely, pon."

"But the reality is that no one's here," Pfle replied.

"The Evil King absolutely exists, pon. The defeat of the Evil King is the game's win condition, pon." Fal twisted three times in midair before returning to the original position. The cloud of golden powder made it difficult to see the black-and-white form. "Your enemy must be somewhere...*somewhere*, pon. Maybe in one of the other areas, pon."

"I'll ask this one more time: the Evil King *must* be inside the game, is that correct?"

"The Evil King absolutely, one hundred percent has to be here, pon. The game was made to be possible to complete, pon."

The Nonako, Rionetta, and Pechka trio was sitting in chairs in the library area. Nonako and Rionetta's expressions were both grim. Pechka figured the look on her own face had to be full of despair, too. They couldn't find the Evil King. The final enemy, the one they absolutely needed to finish the game, was nowhere to be found.

Right now, all the magical girls were searching around again to make sure they hadn't overlooked it somewhere in one of the areas they'd explored so far. Clantail was absent, off helping another team that needed another fighter. Nonako, Rionetta, Pechka, and Nonako's pet dragon were the team in charge of exploring the library area.

The library area was comparatively small. And since they'd scoured this place for the red books needed to unlock the following area, this was also the most thoroughly explored of all the areas. They didn't know what else they could find. They tried searching different places at random, knocking down bookshelves and kicking over the long tables in search of hidden doors and rooms, but they couldn't find any clues anywhere. Tired of searching, they fought monsters instead, but that just wore them out, so the trio ended up just sitting on some chairs and sighing.

"Perhaps the Evil King isn't anywhere," Rionetta said to no one in particular. "Perhaps this game has no Evil King at all, and this quest is all a fool's errand to defeat a nonexistent boss."

"*Mais*, Fal said the Evil King is somewhere," said Nonako.

"Do you *sincerely* believe we can trust that creature?!" Rionetta smacked the table, and the one hit broke the old, tilting piece of furniture in a cloud of dust and wood chips. Then Rionetta kicked the broken table into a bookshelf where it smashed into a mess of countless wood shards on the floor.

Pechka bit back a shriek. Seeing Rionetta storming around frightened her, but she figured that if she made any noise now, Rionetta might get even angrier and turn her rage on Pechka. So she couldn't say anything. Pechka was tired, too, and utterly disheartened at the missing Evil King, but even so, seeing someone angry made her jumpy. In this way, Pechka's cowardice helped her avoid conflict, but she wasn't the only one present.

"Shut up," said Nonako.

"What?" replied Rionetta.

"What does yelling and hitting things solve, *hein*?"

"Well, aren't we self-important?"

"There's nothing good about *négatif* thinking."

"Then why don't you suggest one decent idea? Feel quite free to usher in the Evil King from who-knows-where. Perhaps you could rescue all of us from this place."

"If I could, I'd have already done that, *t'sais*?"

Rionetta stood up. "Your constant pseudo-foreign interjections are driving me perfectly mad."

Not to be defeated, Nonako Miyokata stood up as well. "You have a problem with my *personnalité unique*?"

"I'm saying that attempting to define your personality based on such a trait reveals a terribly *plebeian* character."

"Oh, that's rich, coming from the *charactah* with fake posh *ahticulation, dahling*!"

Rionetta grabbed Nonako by the collar. "You'd do well to consider that my patience is not infinite!"

The pair's voices were swiftly rising in both volume and pitch. Pechka wanted to plug her ears, but she couldn't do that. Conversely, she couldn't stop them, either. She couldn't even burst into tears. All she could manage was to half stand from her chair, flustered and fidgeting.

Rionetta gripped Nonako's collar even harder, wrenching her to her feet, while Nonako grabbed Rionetta's right hand in an attempt to stop her. Rionetta grabbed the interfering wrist with her own left hand, and both of them leaned in close to glare at each another.

Nonako's dragon roared. The sound was unlike that of a bird or beast, a cry of anger that they'd heard many times before in the subterranean area. It roared once, spreading its green wings wide and swooping at the pair. It opened its great maw, lined with rows of sharp fangs, to crunch into Rionetta's right shoulder.

Nonako was startled, and so was Rionetta as she silently shouted with rage. She flailed her right arm, but the dragon wouldn't let go. Nonako ordered the beast to stop, but it didn't seem to hear and kept its fangs in deep. Rionetta smashed her arm and the dragon's head into a bookshelf, but it still wouldn't let go. In fact, it tightened its jaws even more. They could hear something in Rionetta's arm break.

Rionetta screamed and extended the claws on her right hand. Pechka stood up from the chair, and Nonako leaped at Rionetta in an attempt to stop her. But she was too late. Just as she'd done many times before in the subterranean area, Rionetta stroked the dragon's neck with her claws. The weapon she wielded now had higher plus modifications than the ones she'd used back when fighting in the subterranean area, so she cut open the dragon's hard scales like so much papercraft, slicing deep into skin, muscle, fat, blood vessels—everything. Even from where Pechka was standing, she could see how deep the wound was. An instant later, blood was spurting from the gash.

The dragon hit the floor with a thud. Nonako burst into tears as she tried to use a recovery medicine from her magical phone, but it wouldn't work. Rionetta was paler than Nonako, her injured arm dangling as she watched Nonako mashing her magical phone. Rionetta's right sleeve was torn, exposing her arm. The holes in it were equal to the number of the dragon's fangs, and it was even cracked, too. She looked just like a broken and discarded doll.

"Pechka..." Maybe it was just because Pechka thought she looked like a cast-off toy, but Rionetta's voice seemed empty and artificial. She was apparently addressing Pechka, but it sounded like she was just talking to herself. "Will you...come with me?" Rionetta turned to face her. She had to have been looking at Pechka, but her eyes were empty. "I've not at all lived a good life, and I'm not worthy enough to be inviting anyone to join me, but...still..."

Pechka bit her lip hard. She didn't know what she should say or how she should say it. She was trying to think of the thing to say that wouldn't cause conflict or harm to anyone, but she couldn't. She had something to say that might hurt to hear, but she couldn't gather the courage to say it aloud. The determination that had welled up inside her back when they'd fought the knights and robot in the Evil King's castle had long since vanished.

Rionetta looked at Pechka, who replied with neither a yes nor a no and just watched her with tears welling in her eyes.

Rionetta smiled weakly and shook her head. "Good-bye." She

turned away from Pechka. A spray of red mottled her back. Red liquid dripped from her claws. The stench of blood wafted from every inch of her body.

"Wait!" Nonako Miyokata snapped at Rionetta as she began staggering away. "How do you plan to settle this, *hein*?! Don't you dare think you can just run away!"

Rionetta didn't stop. She passed by the fallen chair and kept walking on.

"*Je vais* sue you! You'd better pay damages before you go!" Nonako yelled, red-faced. She'd been holding her dragon until just a moment ago, so her face and shrine maiden outfit were dripping blood. Rionetta didn't stop walking and slowly wobbled away way.

"*Poupée putain!*" Nonako cursed viciously at Rionetta and then ran after her.

Worried that Nonako might hit, kick, or scream at her, Pechka reached out, thinking, *I have to stop her*—and then she noticed the dark shadow on Rionetta's back.

"Watch out!" Pechka's cry seemed to snap Rionetta out of her listless stride, and she sluggishly responded to the fiend's attack, sitting down on a chair a little ways away from the others. She must have sat down hard, as the chair rocked wildly. Rionetta flailed in her seat in an attempt to regain her balance somehow, raising her arms—and then the chair grabbed them. The seat under her transformed into a black angel and flipped them both over, pulling Rionetta from her unstable position to slam her down onto the carpet.

A fiend had transformed into a chair. None of the enemies in this area had done anything like that before. The monsters had always attacked them in a straightforward manner, and the party would beat them up. And when they transformed, they'd only ever turned into living creatures. Come to think of it, the chair Rionetta had sat on had been all by itself. So had one fiend transformed into a chair beforehand to lie in wait while another prepared to attack? Pechka ran after Nonako.

The fiend held Rionetta down while its partner kicked her face as if it were a soccer ball. Once, twice—with the second kick came an awful sound of cracking wood. When the fiend raised its leg to unleash a third kick, Nonako arrived to stab it with her ritual staff. A dark palm stopped her attack, grasping the rod. A wraith had passed through a bookshelf to appear in front of Nonako, blocking her way. The fiend swung its leg down for another soccer kick, and no one was there to stop it as it knocked Rionetta's head violently to one side. The bonnet on her head fluttered into the air.

Pechka put her hand to the holy charm hanging from her neck, clenching it. Since she had this, she could damage the wraith with her attack.

Pechka swung her spatula, and the wraith slipped forward to avoid her strike, then paused and leaned up against Nonako. Wraiths could pass through objects. This still held true with the human body. The wraith sank partway into Nonako's body, and Nonako panicked. She flailed her staff around but failed to connect. The wraith had blinded her with its body.

The fiend responsible for the vicious soccer kicks transformed into a thin, stringlike snake, and passed into the wraith covering Nonako's face. Pechka swung her spatula three times at the wraith, ripping its form to pieces to repel it and remove the blindfold over Nonako's eyes.

Then she smacked the demon holding down Rionetta with her spatula, over and over—*wham wham, wham, wham, wham*—scattering the black shadow.

Rionetta's bonnet had come off because the string under her chin had been cut, but she was still alive. Her disheveled hair swayed this way and that as she got to her feet, pointing behind Pechka, mouth open wide. Pechka turned around. Nonako was there. Her eyes were bulging, lips pressed tight. Blood flowed from the corners of her lips, gushing out from her bloodshot eyes and nose. Her closed lips weakened, and she spat out a clot of blood with a cough before she fell over backward. The thin, stringlike black snake tried to slither out of the red mass, but Rionetta swiped at it with her claws, slicing it into five pieces. It dispersed into a black shadow and disappeared.

Pechka selected a recovery medicine from her magical phone. Her head was all mixed up—she was panicking, confused, and crying—but this one thing, she could manage calmly. The recovery medicine that she'd tried using on Nonako wouldn't work. It was still inside her magical phone. She tried over and over again, but got the same thing. She couldn't use the recovery medicine. Pechka dropped to her knees on the wooden floor. A large splinter stuck in her knee, making it bleed. Her shoulders heaved as she breathed. She didn't want to understand what had just happened.

None of this had ever happened before. A demon transforming into an object to take them by surprise, a wraith using its own body to blindfold them, a fiend infiltrating the body to attack from the inside—none of this had ever happened before.

—Oh. The Evil King's throne.

When the Evil King's throne had been touched, it had brought up some kind of message on their magical phones. It had said something about monster levels. In other words…this?

Pechka heard footsteps and turned toward them. Rionetta was walking away. She'd turned her back on Pechka and Nonako and was trying to leave.

Pechka yelled, "Rionetta!" She didn't know what to say after that. It was just like before. She'd been unable to say anything, and because of that, now Nonako was on the ground. The recovery medicine wasn't working. In other words, she was dead.

Rionetta paused. "Why…? I'm…just…," she muttered and then started walking again. Her head was unsteady, and her bonnet dangled from her right hand, as her left supported her broken arm.

Pechka merely watched her go.

MASTER SIDE #8

"The Evil King isn't there, pon."

"Uh-huh."

"The Evil King isn't there, pon."

The girl tilted her head at a forty-degree angle, eyeing Fal. It was almost impossible to divine Fal's thoughts using only body language. But still, you could get a clue as to what was going on in its mind based on the tone of voice and repetition of the question.

I suppose considering what's going on right now, I don't even really have to guess, the girl thought, returning her head to its original position. Her joints made a loud cracking noise. "You're wrong that the Evil King isn't there." On top of the swivel chair, the girl pulled her knees in and touched the soles of her feet together. "I don't remember ever making them play a game with no Evil King. It'd be physically impossible for the win condition to be the Evil King's defeat if the final boss didn't exist."

"There was no one on the throne, pon."

"Who says the Evil King has to be on the throne? The name 'Evil King's castle' is just a name. Nobody ever said the Evil King would be there—not me, and not you." The girl touched her finger to the desk and flicked it. The swivel chair spun around. "If they can't find their enemy, then it's their fault for failing the task. There's nooo reason to be whining to the master about it. I wouldn't tell them to figure it out right then and there, but the game is made so that they can figure it out after they reach the fake throne. I gave them hints, too. I'm fair. I don't lie or trick people. Unlike *her*."

Gradually, the chair's spinning sped up. Even when it was whirling around so fast that the girl was too blurry to see, her voice remained clear. The junk piled on top of the desk did not get sucked into a vortex, and the chair didn't break, either. It just made odd noises as it twirled along.

"By the way, hasn't Snow White come back?"

Fal was silent and gave no reply to the girl's casual question.

SNOW WHITE SIDE

Snow White had been acting quickly since her return. She didn't need Fal to tell her that she had to hurry. She'd already scanned the list of participants, and two names in particular concerned her. Leaving those two in the game would accelerate the death toll. But having said that, if Snow White interfered directly, the other girls would face the consequences. She couldn't take out the master directly, either. There had been no weaknesses in her heart.

What Snow White *could* do was attack from another angle.

She pulled some strings with an acquaintance who worked in the same division as her, saying she wanted to meet the supervisor of the magical-girl management division. This acquaintance had, in the past, used her magical-girl powers for acts of violence in search of a reward. As long as Snow White had dirt on her, the girl couldn't say no.

The supervisor of the magical-girl management division was a typical old mage, the sort who looked down on the more recently established magical-girl division. No matter how Snow White begged, he would say he was obligated to follow the rules protecting classified information and refuse to tell her anything. He was very proud in his role as a mage, and Snow White would never be able to dig up some weakness of his to use against him, either. She would just be told to go through official channels, and that would be that.

But she wouldn't make it in time that way. She had to get information about the master as quickly as possible. If Snow White's hunch was correct, this mage was the way in.

She was facing the supervisor of the magical-girl management division in a room that was entirely black, save for the mandala-like magical sigils shining in vibrant, varied colors. He was a very stereotypical-looking mage, with a long gray robe that fell to his feet, an impressively long white beard, and a dramatic, twisted staff.

"Please use the official channels," he said.

She'd known he would say that. "That won't make it in time."

"Not my concern."

"Then I'm going to do my own investigation, so please tell me the management division password."

"You think I could tell you that, fool?" His form faded, and he disappeared.

Snow White excused herself from the supervisor's room. She'd gotten the information she needed. When she had requested that the supervisor tell her the password, his thoughts had flowed into her. Right as he'd thought, *I can't let her learn the password*, she'd read a certain sequence of numbers and symbols from his mind.

Now Snow White just had to investigate. She hurried.

CHAPTER 9
THE CHILDREN

☆ **Detec Bell**

Detec Bell rapped on the throne at every quarter-inch interval, but no matter where she hit it, all she heard was the sound of dense, thick marble. There was nothing strange about it. And she'd already investigated everything besides this throne—this room and the room next door, floor to ceiling—and had found nothing. She'd searched anything and everything. Looking at the map, it was clear at a glance that there were no hidden rooms, but still, if there were a tiny space or little crack, there could be an item or message in there.

Detec Bell sighed. Since she'd finished investigating the throne and these rooms, she had to search that stupidly long hallway next.

Once the traps here were activated, they didn't go off a second time. What's more, the Evil King's castle only had what they call "event monsters." Once the knights and jester were defeated, they would not respawn. They'd already confirmed those facts with Fal.

But even if there were no more traps, just thinking about the great length of the hall was daunting.

The other magical girls had headed out to search other areas and would be off running around in search of the Evil King, who had to be around somewhere. The plan was that if anything happened, they'd immediately contact the others, and all the girls would meet up. Seeing that so far, her magical phone had not even twitched, they must not have found anything.

Pfle had been calm. She was not agitated in any recognizable way. It seemed that even with Shadow Gale out of her party, she was still in control. As long as Pfle was calm, it meant that Shadow Gale was probably not going to be up to anything.

Lazuline was making a racket about the situation, but you might say that was par for the course with her. She was getting herself worked up about finding the Evil King and had apparently not yet imagined anything more frightening.

Melville seemed to be one of the calmer ones, too. She was a realist. Detec Bell didn't know what she might get up to later, but she appeared to be of the opinion that now was the time to be searching for the Evil King, since she was cooperating with their search and investigation, as well as helping to defend the other girls. If reality as Melville saw it were to change…Detec Bell didn't know what might happen.

The other magical girls were all right on the brink. One more half step, and they wouldn't be able to function. Clantail only seemed calm because she didn't talk much, and Nokko rarely put forth her own opinions and generally went along with what other people wanted, but both had to be emotionally wrecked. They would be imagining how to escape from this—namely, the most obvious and worst conclusion: that there had never been an Evil King, and that no matter how they struggled, they wouldn't be able to complete the game.

They were like balloons pumped with as much air as they could hold. If anything happened, they'd pop. Detec Bell had been like that until only recently. They all felt helpless, stuck with nowhere to run. They had to let out some air before they all popped. Lazuline's carefree nature had helped Detec Bell do just that. Though it was frustrating to admit, Lazuline was probably a big part of why Detec Bell was feeling more at ease now.

What was needed most now in order to relieve some of the pressure was the Evil King. It didn't even have to be the final boss itself. They just needed a trigger that would lead to some progress, a hint that would guide them to their goal. Even the smallest thing would do.

Detec Bell left the king's throne room, went into the adjoining room, and exited out the other side. The long, long, long, long hallway coiled around and around before her eyes. *I have to investigate all this?* She felt ready for another sigh. But she figured it might be easier for her mentally if she searched the most promising sections rather than combing the whole thing. It was decorated with statues and paintings. Those would be easier to investigate, and it seemed more likely that something would be hidden there instead of in the passage itself.

Then she got an idea. Come to think of it, there was one room in this section she hadn't inspected at all yet.

Carefully examining every one of the decorations in the hallway as she went, Detec Bell made her way toward the area gate. At the halfway point, she turned toward the light pouring in from the outside. It was the area shop.

She stepped out onto the terrace, shielding her eyes from the glaring rays of the sun with her left hand. The air was clearer, somehow—well, it was colder here than inside, which made it seem clearer.

Detec Bell diligently examined the terrace railing, the posts that supported it, everything. There was nothing there. She wiped her forehead. Next, the floor. She investigated the entire surface. Next, the entryway. She studied it with her magnifying glass, knocking lightly on it as she went. Just like with the railing, she found nothing.

...She wasn't done yet.

There was an urn fixed in the center of the railing. From the outside, it looked like an ordinary urn, made of entirely regular ceramic. It was dark inside, and Detec Bell couldn't see anything. She tried sticking her arm in, but she couldn't touch the bottom. Even after straining her fingertips as far as they would go, she still couldn't reach.

She thought about breaking it, too, but before that, she activated her magical phone and clicked USE SHOP. Scrolling down the list of items, she stopped on the very last one. There was an item listed there that she'd never seen before. She was baffled, confused, shocked, and then finally, exuberant. She hadn't even considered that there would be a new item for sale.

But when she checked the description of the new item, she was puzzled again. Her newfound joy faded a bit. Written on the screen was MEMORY RESTORATION DEVICE.

Memory Restoration Device?

She knew what the words meant. What she didn't understand was what the item actually did. Come to think of it, when they'd touched the throne, she recalled that they'd gotten some message about memories. Did it have to do with that?

It was priced cheaply. It was the least expensive of all the items for sale in the Evil King's castle shop—by a long shot. Detec Bell purchased the Memory Restoration Device and immediately activated it. It was an application. Maybe it was a clue that would help them in their search for the Evil King. She had a powerful suspicion that something extremely important was in front of her.

WILL YOU RESTORE THE LOST MEMORIES? This message appeared on the screen along with the option to select YES or NO. *Will you restore the lost memories, or not?*

Detec Bell didn't understand what that sentence meant. She tilted her head, and that was when fireworks exploded before her eyes.

Something had happened. She didn't know what. Her cheeks were cold. And not just her cheeks. Her lips, right arm, body, and right leg were all chilly, too. Not just cold. Something felt hard. Slowly, as her head began to clear, she got a grasp on her situation. The chill, the hardness—this was marble. She'd fallen on the stone floor.

She tried to get up, but her body wouldn't move. Only her right hand, hidden underneath her cape, just barely moved. She could see the white marble floor before her eyes turning red here and there. Without even thinking about it, she understood what it was. Her head ached like it was being squeezed in a vise. Something was flowing from it.

Footsteps reverberated from the marble floor. Someone was approaching. They came right up to her and then stopped. She sensed someone was there. Were they the one? Had they struck her and knocked her to the ground? That wasn't a monster. She didn't know who it was, but she could tell it was a magical girl. Detec Bell tried to make sense of all the thoughts in her head.

Why had she been targeted? Who had done it? What for? What had she been doing right before she'd was hit? She couldn't hand over her magical phone or its contents. Wait. Was she going to die? She didn't want to die. But. Would she? Still make it in time, at least? She had to make it. Could she? Use it. Her magic. The buildings in this game would not oppose their master. They wouldn't answer Detec Bell's questions. But they could still talk to her. They just wouldn't answer if she asked. Still. Even if it wouldn't work. Somehow.

Someone had struck her. She didn't know who. Her consciousness was fading. If the one who hit her took her items, it would all have been for nothing. She had to give this to the one person she could trust most.

Still facedown, Detec Bell kissed the ground and moved her right hand.

☆ Nokko

An event is now beginning. Players, please gather in the wasteland town square.

At first, they were surprised it was already that time. Next came feelings of relief.

In the two hours since they'd reached the fake throne, all of the magical-girl players had joined together in search of the abominable Evil King. The atmosphere was tense, set to explode, and all their eyes were sparkling. *Where is the Evil King? If we can just find him, the game will be over.*

Even if she attempted to calm everyone down, Nokko was near her emotional limits, too. Her heart was racing, her breaths came shallow and quick, and she couldn't stop the cold sweat coming from her pores. She couldn't influence the others well when she was like this.

She was part of the team in charge of the city area, so the monsters weren't that strong, and since Clantail was guarding her, she didn't have to feel uneasy about battles. Her anxiety had a different source. Clantail was terribly irritated and had been stomping her hooves over every little thing.

For a long, long time, every second feeling like an hour, they patrolled the area, suffering, exhausted. And then, there was an announcement.

The premaintenance period event involved a forcible summons. Even if they didn't want to participate, they had no choice. Once the time came, no matter where they were, they were transferred to the square in the wasteland town, so the event was unavoidable.

All the magical girls gathered in the square seemed tired. That was understandable.

"Huh?" Lazuline made a confused noise. "Where's Bell?" They looked at one another. Detec Bell wasn't there.

"...And Nonako?" Clantail muttered softly. Detec Bell wasn't the only one missing. Nonako Miyokata and her dragon were both absent from the square.

"Actually, it looks like she's not in the wasteland area at all." Lazuline was checking Detec Bell's position on her phone's map application. Only three of their party members were displayed: Nokko, Lazuline, and Pfle. Detec Bell alone was missing.

"Nonako was..." Pechka, so pale she looked ready to faint at any moment, began telling them what happened, her eyes fixed on a single point on the ground. She wobbled more than once as she explained, and Clantail moved to support her halfway through. At times, Pechka glanced toward Rionetta, too, but she was facing away, not even attempting to look at Pechka.

The monsters in the library area had assaulted them using entirely new tactics. They'd launched a surprise attack—one had turned into a chair, a wraith had used its own body as a blindfold, and another monster had transformed into a tiny snake to invade Nonako's body. Pechka said that this had killed Nonako.

Clantail bared her clenched teeth. Pechka no longer seemed about to pass out and instead looked like she was on the verge of death. As the one supporting her, Clantail couldn't stamp her hooves or yell or vent any of her feelings, and the rage was showing itself on her face. By the time Pechka had finally finished the whole story, standing had become difficult for her, and Clantail lowered her to sit on the fountain side.

Pfle nodded. "The dragons in the subterranean area have become curiously more coordinated as well. It must be for the same reasons."

Melville, too, talked about the goblins in the mountain area and how they were working together in a way they hadn't before.

And those machines that had spawned in the city area, too—the group had beaten them down with their charms and high-powered weapons and armor, so Nokko hadn't realized it, but reflecting on it more closely, she got the feeling that the monsters had acted differently than during their previous encounters in the area.

"So what about Bell?" Lazuline looked each of the magical girls in the eye in turn. Nokko met her gaze and dropped her head reflexively.

Lazuline turned on her magical phone. "Falzey, tell me, please. Where's Bell?"

For a second, the image of Fal was streaked with noise, a distortion like TV static that then turned into a dust of golden flakes. Then Fal began to speak as if nothing had happened. "The premaintenance period event is mandatory, pon. After a certain amount of time has passed, any magical girl who has failed to arrive at the square will be forcibly transported to the square, pon. If any magical girl does not appear here, it means she is no longer playing the game, pon."

"What's that s'posed to mean?" Lazuline asked.

Fal's reply was quiet. "It's highly likely...that she's dead, pon."

Lazuline stomped hard on the ground. "There's no way! She was in charge of investigatin' the Evil King's castle. *You're* the one who said no more monsters would spawn there, right?!"

"That's exactly right, pon. There will be no more monsters in the Evil King's castle area, pon."

"So then Bell can't be dead. There's no way for her to die in the Evil King's castle when there's no monsters there and we already set off all the traps!"

"I will now begin explaining the event, pon."

"Listen up! Hey! I'm asking you where Bell went!"

A gust of wind blew into the square, sweeping up sand. The girls covered their faces with their hands. The breeze passed, the sand settled, and Fal began describing the event. It was as if the wind had carried away Lazuline's questions with it.

"This event...um, since you've made it to the end of the Evil King's castle, this won't be the usual random event, but a special one...pon. Allow me to distribute a strategy guide for you all. Everyone, please pull out your magical phones, pon." It didn't seem like Fal was taking his time explaining on purpose, and yet he was speaking rather slowly. It was as if even Fal hadn't been aware of this event.

"Wot's th' meanin' innit now?"

"Melvy is wondering why you'd hand out strategy guides at this point," Lazuline translated, "and that bothers me, too. But more importantly, what happened to Bell?!"

"There, it's been distributed. All right, this event is now over, pon." A strategy guide application was now installed on Nokko's phone. When she launched it, it displayed a message.

"I don't care about this thing! What's important is Bell!"

"Hold on, Lazuline." Pfle restrained the other girl, who was ready to dash off. Everyone who'd checked their strategy guides was frozen.

Now that you have reached the throne, you have earned the right to know the secret of the Evil King. The truth is that the Evil King is among the players. She acts in secret for the sake of her own victory condition: killing all other players. Take care not to be killed.

The message was so direct that Nokko felt its impact like a slam to the head. Everything in her mind turned into a tangled mess, and her knees started trembling. It seemed like everyone else was talking about something, but Nokko couldn't hear it.

Pfle clapped her hands together. "The event is over, which means we're not obliged to remain in the square. We should all search for Detec Bell. Avoid going alone. Be sure to keep to groups of three or more...to stay safe, no matter who the Evil King might be."

Before Pfle had even finished talking, Lazuline had raced off with Melville and Clantail close behind.

☆ Shadow Gale

The interval between the premaintenance event and logout was very short. Ultimately, it was nothing more than a little additional time or an extra break, not enough to be used on anything productive.

Following after Lazuline, who had taken the lead, Shadow Gale dashed off to the Evil King's castle. Once she reached the castle, she launched Pfle's map application and checked for the four icons of her party members. Pfle's own icon, as well as Nokko's, was at the entrance to the Evil King's castle. Then there was Lazuline's, and one more icon that had to be Detec Bell. Those icons were on the terrace of the castle, in the shop zone.

Were they okay for time? Shadow Gale could probably still make it. Wordlessly, she ran with all her strength, her footsteps pounding across the marble floor. She arrived at the terrace, and when she passed through the entrance, her toes touched liquid. A familiar smell hit her nostrils. It was the same thing she'd smelled back when they'd logged in after the end of the first maintenance period…when she'd discovered Masked Wonder, murdered.

A pool of blood had spread across the white marble floor, and in its center was Lapis Lazuline, hunched over on her knees, with Rionetta, Clantail, and Melville standing around her. Clantail was facing away from Shadow Gale, toward the outside. Her tail was hanging limp. Rionetta's head drooped, expressionless, while Melville was shaking her head at the four magical girls who had come in. "'M sorry," she said.

Lazuline's shoulders were shaking. She knelt in the center of the pool, trembling and heedless of the blood soaking her blue costume as she clutched something. Shadow Gale could see shoes, knee socks, a pale gray cape, a limply dangling arm, and a broken magnifying glass. It was Detec Bell. Her head was crushed, a mess of white and red. That was clearly what had killed her.

Her costume was in disarray, too, and not just because she'd fallen. Her coat had been shredded, her cap ripped, and her shirt and skirt rolled up. The disheveled state of her clothes suggested the killer had been looking for something.

They were all speechless, staring at Detec Bell's gruesome transformation.

"I'm supposed to hand it to the blue magical girl, right?"

Shadow Gale lifted her head at the sudden, unfamiliar voice and looked toward Pfle. Pfle also seemed startled, looking back at her. Shadow Gale scanned the terrace. Clantail turned back toward them, Rionetta lifted her head, Pechka seemed frightened, and Nokko was readying her mop. Melville had faded away, melting into the white of the marble. Still cradling Detec Bell, Lazuline skittered backward without rising from her knees, placing her back to the wall as she glanced cautiously around her.

It hadn't been any of them. That voice hadn't belonged to a magical girl or Fal. It was more human, like the voice of a middle-aged man. No one in the game so far could have talked like that.

"Could you move aside?" That same voice again. Shadow Gale sensed something odd at her feet and looked down to see a giant face. She panicked and leaped back. The other magical girls also moved off the face. With the weight gone, the enormous visage made an expression of relief and breathed out a *phew.* For a human face on the floor, it was rather cartoonish in style and expression. But despite that, this whole area was covered in a pool of blood, inevitably including the stylized features, which just made the sight especially grotesque. Shadow Gale winced.

The face, which resembled a middle-aged man from an anime or manga, goggled its eyes around, looking at all the alarmed magical girls. It must have had a thought, then, as it blew out another *phew* and started talking. "I can't give you any hints." Its big eyes swiveled around and looked toward Detec Bell, still in Lazuline's arms. "But I'll do a favor if I'm asked, at least. She said to hand this to the magical girl in blue." The face sucked in its cheeks, pouted its lips, and spat something out from inside. The object rolled through the pool of blood, trailing a line of fluid that was probably saliva behind it until it thunked to a halt at Lazuline's feet. It was a magical phone.

"Good-bye, then." The bulges and dips on the floor disappeared, its outline faded, and everything that had made up the giant face vanished. All that was left was the white marble floor, a great deal of blood, and the magical phone, soiled with saliva and blood.

Unfazed by the spit and blood, with Detec Bell still cradled in her right arm, Lazuline reached out to take the magical phone in her left hand and turned it on. It activated. It had probably seen some pretty rough treatment, but it apparently wasn't broken. "This is...Bell's magical phone, isn't it?"

Detec Bell's magical phone had come out of the mouth of a giant face? Pfle sighed on Shadow Gale's back. It tickled the hairs on the back of her neck, and it felt gross.

"Detec Bell's magic was to converse with buildings," said Pfle. "Does anyone know how she exercised her magic?"

"Bell told me that she'd kiss a building and talk with the face that popped up there. But she complained that she couldn't use her magic inside the game."

"Strictly speaking, I'd wager it wasn't that she couldn't use it, but rather that she couldn't get any information from the buildings," Pfle said, thinking aloud. She might have been watching the other magical girls' reactions as she did. "That would explain what that large face just said. But it seems that even if she couldn't get information out of the buildings here, they would still do her favors. And the favor she asked was to hand this magical phone to you, Lazuline."

Lazuline was staring hard at the magical phone in her grasp.

"Detec Bell chose to use her magic to entrust her phone to the face and even indicated who should receive it—which means there's someone else she *didn't* want having it. Look, her clothing is in disarray. Most likely, someone was trying to steal her magical phone. But they failed." All of them held their breaths, listening intently to Pfle as she spoke.

"We can hypothesize two things at this point. First, the one who attempted to steal her phone was not a monster. It was probably one of the players, the one who killed her—the Evil King." Someone let out a tiny yelp. "The other thing is that important information is hidden within that magical phone. It's so important that, despite knowing she was about to die, Detec Bell still tried to leave it to Lazuline—to us."

Pfle used her phone to launch her magic carpet. She dropped from Shadow Gale's back onto the carpet and looked up at the sky. "We don't have much time." The sun was still sparkling brilliantly, but in the game, sunset was sudden. Intuitively, Shadow Gale knew that it was close to setting. In other words, she could tell that the logout time was almost upon them.

Pfle took the magical phone from Lazuline and lowered her carpet by a foot, almost all the way to the ground, so that everyone could see the screen. She began tapping through the magical phone. She checked her party members, amount of candy in her possession, her address book, messages, Internet browsing history, memo pad, and then finally stopped on her item list. "What's this?"

The Memory Restoration Device. Shadow Gale had never seen this item before. From Detec Bell's history, they could see it had been bought at the shop in the Evil King's castle. Pfle launched the application and inspected its contents.

WILL YOU RESTORE LOST MEMORIES? YES OR NO.

"What does this mean?" Pfle pressed YES with her finger. The lighting behind the NO disappeared, and the YES shone white. A message appeared on the screen:

Memories have been turned on. The players' lost memories will be restored as of the beginning of the next maintenance period.

The time had come. The sun turned to shadow, Shadow Gale's awareness faded, and then she was sitting on her bed in her own room as Mamori Totoyama. Kanoe was in front of her. She was sitting in Mamori's chair, just like she had been before they'd logged in to the game again.

Suddenly, the inside of her head was as bright and clear as day. The haze disappeared, and all her memories were back. Mamori bent over and vomited again and again onto the floor.

☆ Pechka

Chika's memories returned, and she took two days off from school.

The battle in the Evil King's castle had been fierce. The enemies had been strong, and most of all, there'd been a lot of them. Missiles flying, explosions, sounds that made her want to plug her ears, and choking smoke. The knights' sword swings had made her arm go numb when she blocked them with her shield. Despite its high plus modifications, it couldn't entirely block the enemies' weapons.

Pechka's burdensome presence had meant that Clantail and Rionetta couldn't fight how they wanted and were forced to focus on defending her while she cowered behind them, knees trembling and shield up. She hadn't been doing anything in particular; she'd just been there to be protected. She had made excuses for herself, telling herself that if she fought, she'd only get in the way. She had been fine with being the protected, doing hardly anything.

The turning point had come quickly. Right in the middle of the fight, a bright, red-hot magma had welled in her heart, swallowing up everything. It engulfed her fear, fretting, anguish, aversion to combat, and everything else, and turned it into loathing for her enemies and a desire to protect her allies, and Pechka had moved to the front line.

Now that Pechka was able to protect herself, Rionetta and Clantail weren't so pressed. That was the point when they broke the enemy's line like water bursting through a dam. In the end, the magical girls were victorious, and they didn't lose anyone. Considering how strong their enemies had been, it was a miracle.

Thinking back on it after it was over paralyzed Pechka with fear, but during the fight, she'd been in a trance, blocking the enemies' attacks with her shield and swinging her spatula left and right. An enemy had dodged her attack then evaded her counterattack, so next, she bashed it with her shield. Maybe she hadn't been in a trance. She must have been enjoying herself. It was fun to fight her enemies in order to protect her allies, these people who were so important to her.

Their next fight had been the one in the library area. Again and again, she'd swung her spatula at the fiend that had been holding down Rionetta. She'd used it to beat away the wraith that had been blinding Nonako. She didn't even want to think about what had happened in the end, but even so, in that moment, Pechka had felt exhilarated. When she'd been attacking the enemies, there hadn't been anything else in her head except *Get away from my friends!* She hadn't even thought to be scared or frightened.

That was right. Pechka hadn't always been so afraid of fighting. It was true that she wasn't any good at it. Her magic was to make good food, so she didn't have any special physical abilities. She'd never trained nor practiced. But still, she hadn't been so bad that she would bench herself and watch everyone else fight their hardest. She'd known to fight when she had to, and doing it had made her feel great.

Why had Pechka come to avoid battles? Why couldn't she move her feet and step up to the front, even in a crisis situation? Now she remembered why.

"Yeah, it's good," Ninomiya was saying, stuffing his cheeks with his first box lunch from her in two days. "Man, it *really* is, you know?" It sounded like he was asking one of his guy friends to agree with him, and though it felt a little funny, she nodded anyway. Ninomiya smiled, too, and his friendly grin pricked at Pechka's heart painfully.

She understood why she was so drawn to him. He was very much like someone she'd once known. He was so cool and strong when he played sports. He put in his best effort for the sake of his future, and he was never lazy or slacking off. But he also liked to talk, and when he smiled, he seemed so friendly. Even the way he enjoyed Pechka's cooking and showered her with compliments—*So good! So good!*—was just like her.

A familiar voice sounded in Pechka's mind, the voice of a dear friend who was now gone.

Damn, you're such a crybaby, Pechka.

It's not worth crying over at all. You always think that all you have to do is burst into tears!

She'd said some pretty harsh things to Pechka, too.

Relax. As long as I'm here, you won't get a scratch. So stop crying—seriously. All that wailing really makes me uncomfortable.

Hey, Pechka, that wasn't so bad. That last kick was half-decent.

They'd always been together.

Cut this out, you guys! Open your eyes! How can you all just lie down and take orders from her?! This stuff isn't okay!

Run, Pechka!

Right up until the end, they'd been together.

To Chika, she'd been nothing more than another classmate. She was always making lame jokes and fooling around with her friends, and even though Chika thought privately that she was annoyingly loud, she didn't have the courage to scold the other girl to her face. To her, Chika had surely been no more than one of the crowd. She'd been pretty popular in their class, so she maybe she didn't even notice Chika. Her clique was good at sports and liked being active, while Pechka's preferred books and always occupied the same spot in the library at lunch hour. The two had nothing in common, aside from being in the same class.

During the school field trip, they'd been set up as a pair for the walk through a "haunted forest" by drawing straws, and at the time, both of them had probably been annoyed. Chika saw her as just plain loud and tactless, while she saw Chika as a bland and boring girl who had nothing in common with her. They couldn't have fun together like friends, and there was no excitement like there would have been between a girl-boy pair. It was the most boring combination.

Though the test of courage should have ended with little fanfare, her adventurous spirit got the better of her, and she had suggested that they go off the arranged path to take a shortcut, leading the outing to an unusual conclusion.

Chika had desperately tried to stop her, begging her not to, but an outdoorsy girl brimming with a healthy spirit of adventure wasn't about to listen to an indoor type's attempts at persuasion. Ponytail swaying, she gallantly marched out into the bush, and Chika, who didn't want to be left behind, reluctantly followed after her.

The shortcut was nothing but the vestiges of a deer trail, meandering and not at all in a straight line, and before they knew it, they were both alone in the middle of the woods, and neither of them knew where they should go anymore. Chika cried and blamed her companion for her thoughtlessness, while the other girl put on a tough act, striding forward steadily and insisting this was no big deal. She walked and walked, stubbornly pushing forward until they emerged at a clearing.

The tiny little house that looked like either a mountain cabin or a ruin was sitting there all alone. Figuring it might be occupied, the two of them ran toward it, and then, once they were a bit closer, they realized someone was standing on the roof.

In the silent forest, void of any sound from insects, birds, or beasts, they heard a flute. The clear tune was sucked into the starry sky. The figure on the roof was playing the flute. It was a common children's song, but the sight was so fantastical, it captured their hearts. Maybe the reason the insects and birds were silent was in reverence of the instrument. In something of a dreamlike state, the two of them gazed up at the roof, standing silently until the tune was done and utter silence had fallen once more.

Chika's breath caught in her throat. It was a very beautiful woman.

Her blouse was decorated with frills. Over it, she wore a jacket the color of fresh green grass with a rose design. An amber collar pin held it in the front. Her translucent-white thighs were boldly exposed, her legs lithe and slender, while multicolored roses bloomed in the vines that wound around all over her soft-looking, artlessly tied golden hair. The bloom at one of her shoulders was particularly large, a red-purple rose as big as a baby's head. Her facial features were flawless, and her eyes were bright red. In the darkness, the only light came from Chika's flashlight, and yet even though the woman's face wasn't well illuminated, her beauty had been visible.

Most of all, those ears. Just like the forest people, the elves in the fantasy novels that Chika had once read, the pointed tips were poking out of hair that failed to hide them.

"Good evening." Her voice sounded so pleasant in Chika's ears. It was an ordinary greeting, but it twined about her body and soul. "I am the Musician of the Forest, Cranberry. I am a magical girl."

* * *

The samurai girl Pechka had met in the game had said, "Must I do this again? Is it not over?"

She'd also said, "Is it not over? Come on, Musician."

Musician. The Musician of the Forest, Cranberry. The name floated up in her mind. Her lost memories returned.

The reason Pechka hated fighting was that she had never fought to protect her friends. She'd fought to protect herself *from* her friends.

Everyone had accepted the game so naturally. Even after they'd learned that dying in the game meant death in real life, while she had cried and wailed she'd also thought, *Oh. I knew it.*

The strategy guide Fal had distributed to them during the last event had said "the Evil King is among the players." One of her friends, one of the magical girls, was the Evil King.

"Thanks for the food!" Ninomiya put down the chopsticks.

Pechka accepted the box back from him and smiled. "It's my pleasure." She stood up, approached Ninomiya, and gently kissed his cheek. When she drew back, his mouth was half-open, his eyes wide as he stared at her. Pechka gave him a toothy grin. "See you later, then." She turned from the shocked, speechless boy and dashed away.

☆ Shadow Gale

Mamori was lying on her back in bed, a thin blanket draped over her. After regurgitating everything in her stomach, she felt a little better. But the nausea hadn't gone away entirely.

Kanoe was sitting in the chair, watching Mamori.

"I remember now," said Mamori.

"Yes, me too."

"I didn't want to remember it, though."

"Indeed. Neither did I."

The Musician of the Forest, Cranberry. The examiner from the time Mamori and Kanoe had become magical girls. A total of 104 candidates had gathered from nations all over the world for that magical-girl selection exam. Their examiner had been surprised, saying that such a large-scale selection exam was unprecedented, and her sidekick had happily claimed that it would surely be an amazing exam, pon. Had that exam really been unprecedented, though, or had it just been utterly mundane to Cranberry?

"It finally makes sense," said Kanoe.

"What…makes sense?"

"I never forget the things I've seen. Even people I've only ever encountered in passing. I'll always remember, once I've heard their names. But I couldn't remember the name of our examiner, and furthermore, I didn't see anything strange about that. Our memories about Musician of the Forest, Cranberry, and the exam that she oversaw must have been erased—by someone."

Mamori rolled over toward the wall, turning her back to Kanoe. "Oh."

Kanoe had nursed Mamori and cleaned up her vomit as well. Maybe she'd done it because she figured that ordering someone else to would've caused a big fuss, and then Mamori would be quarantined and they wouldn't be able to see each other. Mamori considered making a crack to the effect of, *I must be the first and last person to ever make you clean up puke, miss,* but she didn't have the energy to say it aloud.

Right now, she'd rather not look at Kanoe, if she had the option. It would make Mamori remember, whether she wanted to or not, what had happened during that exam and what she herself had done. There was nothing left for her to throw up but acid.

"But anyhow," Kanoe went on, "I've figured out the culprit."

"Yeah…me too."

"I understand now why I failed, too." Kanoe sounded calm and collected. She would not lose control like Mamori. Even now that she remembered what she'd done, what she'd been forced to do to become a magical girl, she was still the same old Kanoe Hitokouji: strong, indomitable, and proud. "I'd estimated that simply examining character, not motive or opportunity, would enable me to figure out the culprit. And that judgment was based on experience—founded on the supposition that if a magical girl were to commit a crime, she would use her magic to conceal her motive and opportunity as best she could, and so I judged that I should examine character only. In both the wasteland town square and the Great Dragon's cavern, I observed their reactions…and failed. The culprit used magic to conceal her methods and falsify her facial expressions, disguising even her own character."

Kanoe's voice turned cheerful. "Well, this was all before our memories were restored. I understand now what it is she wanted to steal, even if it meant killing Detec Bell. With our memories returned, she's painted into a corner. We have a clue that one of us is suspicious, and if you go from there and consider her methodology, you'll naturally come to see what she did and how…the way she concealed the Miracle Coin and manipulated Cherna Mouse's candy stock. I don't even have to show off and play the great detective, explaining to everyone, *'So-and-so is the culprit, and this is how she did the crime!'* Even the ones who don't understand how she did it will have a vague sense of who it is…since they have their memories back."

"Yeah…I'm sure you're right."

"We can't let our guards down around her, even seven-on-one. But it will be concerning if she kills us one by one before we can meet up. We'll gather the others as quickly as possible so as to avoid that. According to the message, she is the Evil King. Once we defeat her, the game will be over."

"Yeah."

"I registered you in our party right before our last session ended. You, Lazuline, Nokko, and I will already be together from the moment we log in. But how quickly will the rest be able to convene after that? Worst case scenario, one or two will die."

"You think some will die?"

"I want to avoid that, if possible, but our enemy must realize that she'll be under suspicion. She will act. Well, even if some die, we'll minimize the losses. After that, we avoid contact with the enemy for three days. Then, when we're forced together for the premaintenance event, that's when we hit her." The chair creaked. It sounded like Kanoe had stood. "The next login is in two days and twenty-two hours. Until then, rest up." Mamori heard her walking on the carpet. The door opened, then closed. Mamori rolled over onto her back.

Kanoe never changed. Not last time, and not this time.

Even among a crowd of a hundred, Pfle was still Pfle. She occasionally formed alliances, occasionally broke them, and occasionally caused conflict, all the while manipulating the magical girls like an orchestra conductor. She occupied many positions: the agitator who sent them to their deaths, a double-dealing fraudster, their reliable leader, or a heroic martyr. She watched them from above as she maneuvered her pawns, sometimes becoming one herself, tilting the scales, pulling the strings.

Even in an aberrant situation, a battle royal, she had made full use of her talent, crushing every one of the other magical-girl candidates, deceiving them, killing them, or making them kill.

The last one, her ally throughout her ordeal, she'd shot in the back. The girl's limbs had blown away, and her organs had dangled from a tree branch. Blood literally rained down while Pfle conversed with the forest musician, who had been watching them from the shadow of the trees. Pfle's face, hands, clothes, everything had been soaked red—not in her own blood. It was the blood of her sacrifice.

"In accord with our contract," said Pfle. "You should have nothing to complain about here."

"What a wonderful show. I would personally request a match with you," Cranberry replied.

"That would be counter to our agreement. My swindling and cajolery isn't the strength you seek, anyway. If you're looking for a rival, go elsewhere."

Kanoe had looked over at Mamori. Her handsome face had warped for an instant, and then immediately went back to a smile. "Shall we go, then? I really am somewhat tired."

Mamori had been totally ignorant. She hadn't been told of this secret contract Kanoe had made with the Musician of the Forest, or what it was about. When Kanoe had mentioned that this was "in accord with a contract," Mamori had wondered if she would be killed. She thought that perhaps, if Kanoe's contract were fulfilled, Shadow Gale's death might be a part of it, and that had probably revealed itself on her face. And Kanoe had noticed that look.

The change on Kanoe's face had not been anger or disappointment, but sadness. She hadn't even considered that Mamori might worry that Kanoe would kill her. Mamori's baseless fears had wounded Kanoe. That was the first time Mamori had ever seen Kanoe look hurt and then try to hide it. She'd never seen her do that since, either.

Mamori figured their secret contract might have something to do with allowing two people to pass. Kanoe had made Cranberry an offer on the condition that two would pass the exam. Either money, or something in the exam—just something. The question was: What about now?

Had Masked Wonder been forced to do the same thing? A battle royal?

Mamori rubbed her eyes with her sleeve. The pillowcase under her head was wet, too. Surely, even with her back turned, Kanoe had noticed she was crying.

MASTER SIDE #9

Once, there was a magical girl named Cranberry.

At her selection exam, when she was still very small, there had been an accident. One of the participants had lost control of her magic, and the examiner failed to stop it. It had killed the examiner and all the participants but Cranberry. They said the cause of the accident had been a flaw in the mascot Fav's functions, which kept things in check.

They also said that afterward, Fav had taken Cranberry, still suffering from psychological wounds, and tempted her, driving her to violence.

This girl thought that was nonsense. They were just blaming it all on the mascot and cutting off nothing but the lizard's tail, weren't they?

The accident had been due to a deficiency in the system. Cranberry had become an examiner because they'd failed to take the proper precautions and their checks had been lenient, too. They were trying to create something noble: magical girls. But they were far too careless with the selection process, and that was precisely what caused this sort of thing.

As an examiner, Cranberry had acquired a position where she

could select magical girls. Exams were held at her discretion, and the content of these tests had been secret. Cranberry had set the participants in her exams to killing one another, even participating personally to intensify the experience. Then, if a winner remained, she overwrote their memories with fake ones of having passed a regular magical-girl selection exam. Those battle royals had been extremely appalling, and it had not been uncommon for them to end with no victor at all. At the time, the people of the Magical Kingdom had praised Cranberry's rigorous spirit for holding such demanding examinations and had not suspected her.

The roots of Cranberry's crimes dug deep. She'd had many accomplices aside from her sidekick. This was the reason that her battle-royal selection exams had not been exposed until the one that would be her last, when the examinees had turned the tables on her, and Snow White had exposed her deeds. Until this scandal had come to light, she'd been hailed as a great magical girl. Some had even deified her.

No, even after her wicked deeds were exposed, some continued to worship her.

Even after Cranberry's death, there had been two examiners who still believed in the insane logic Cranberry had espoused, that only the strong were worthy of becoming magical girls. They had been following in her footsteps until the magical girl in white, Snow White, had unmasked them. The two main reasons Snow White had come to be called the "magical-girl hunter" were that she had exposed that pair, and that she had called Cranberry to task for her crimes.

But the bespectacled girl believed Snow White was not being hard enough.

The examiners influenced by her evil deeds were not the only seeds Cranberry had sown. She had been a very active examiner over a long period of time. Because of her exams, the world was now awash with magical girls who were strong and nothing else, girls who had no qualms about kicking others down, who had won the role of magical girl by bloodying their hands, killers, ignorant of the value of life.

They should not have been chosen. Cranberry was the wrong examiner, and she'd chosen the wrong magical girls. No matter if you erased their memories, no matter how much work they did—at the core, they were not the right kind of magical girls.

That was why there was a need for reexamination. But the Magical Kingdom had just let them be. The higher-ups took the girls to be Cranberry's victims. They hadn't even returned their memories, much less questioned their sins. They'd merely let sleeping dogs lie so the problem wouldn't grow any bigger.

It was bullshit. Just what did they think magical girls were?

Magical girls were kind. They understood the pain of strangers, and they could think with empathy. They were bold, but they would abhor the idea of killing one another. They were hardworking, smart and physically capable, filled with a sense of justice, and charming. A wise magical girl like that would be able to seek out the Evil King and defeat them.

For bringing up the Cranberry incident, turning her back on the will of the Magical Kingdom, and carrying out her own exam, this girl would be hated, shunned, and loathed. She was okay with that. It was enough for her if she could just pick out the righteous ones from among "Cranberry's children"—though that would only happen if any of them were actually righteous at all. Most of them were not. They were all like Magical Daisy, cocky because she'd gotten an anime based on her life despite being ignorant of her own origins.

If they died, then that was as it should be. It would simply mean that they were the wrong sort of magical girl. The right kind would definitely survive—because the gods would choose them.

CHAPTER 10
PECHKA IN CREATUREWORLD

☆ **Pechka**

The real world had been cloudy for the whole maintenance period, with the chance of precipitation hovering between 50 and 70 percent. It had been a while since Pechka had last seen the sun, but regardless, now it did nothing for her. This sun had only been created for the purpose of illumination and didn't stir any emotions in her. Same with the blowing wind and haze of dust. They had no meaning beyond serving as part of the backdrop.

Pechka squatted, stood, squatted, and stood again, pushing off her knees with her hands to get a good stretch.

Now logged in to the game again, Pechka was in the wasteland area, waiting for Clantail. Their habits were not going to change, even now that their memories were back. Her magical phone chirped, so she checked it. There was a message from Pfle.

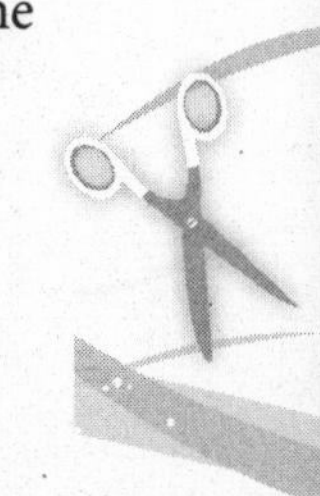

This is Pfle. I want to convene. Tell me where you are and keep an eye on your surroundings.

Pechka wanted to meet up, too. She replied with her current location.

She launched the map application on her phone. It displayed three icons in the wasteland area: Clantail, Pechka, and Rionetta. Both Clantail and Rionetta were headed her way. It would be better to wait here rather than wander off somewhere herself.

As the wind threatened to blow away her hat, Pechka held it down with her left hand, breathing a sigh. Rionetta's icon was there. She was relieved the other girl hadn't unregistered from their party.

It wasn't long before she heard hooves. Someone was racing toward her, kicking up dust. It was Clantail.

There were things Pechka wanted to talk about—namely what had happened before. There'd been so much at once, one thing after another, and she hadn't been able to tell Clantail the whole story about Nonako. She and Rionetta had had a big fight, but even after that, Nonako had fought to protect Rionetta, and Pechka wanted to tell Clantail that. She also wanted to discuss the memories they'd regained.

Clantail stopped just over ten yards away from Pechka. Even at a distance, she seemed a little thin. Her cheeks had been rounder before the maintenance period. Her expression was hard. Her right hand floated halfway between reaching out to Pechka and dangling slack. Pechka was about to call out to her, but Clantail spoke first. She sounded like she was trying to keep her voice from trembling. "Lower your weapon."

Pechka watched Clantail in puzzlement. But Clantail wasn't looking at her. Her gaze was trained on something behind her.

Pechka got a whiff of roses, and something cold touched her neck. She felt metal, and the smell of tempered iron passed through her nostrils, along with the clinging scent of blood. Before Pechka could move a muscle, she was snatched by the back of her collar, flung around like so much cloth or paper, and slammed into the ground. Her magical phone rolled out from her pocket. She failed to catch her fall, and her back hit the ground hard enough to knock the wind out of her. She opened and closed her mouth soundlessly, unable to inhale.

The sun was at her attacker's back, and its powerful glare obscured her expression from view. But Pechka could discern the outfit of the magical girl who'd thrown her: her pointed ears, winding vines, large roses, longbow, and javelins.

"Dinnae come nae closer." She wasn't talking to Pechka. That remark was for Clantail. She had been running up to try to save Pechka, and Melville was ordering her to stay away. "Git ye back." Melville's javelin was pointed at Pechka's chin.

Pechka couldn't make a sound. She couldn't cry for help or run away—and not because her breath was gone. She was too frightened to move. *I'll do it now, I'll do it now*, she told herself, but when the moment came, she just trembled, unable to act.

She was unbearably terrified of the magical girl behind her and her casual acts of violence. But more than the viciousness itself, it was those vines, those roses, and those pointed ears that inspired such fear in Pechka. She remembered now—the one who'd forced them all into a bloodbath, the Musician of the Forest, Cranberry. Melville looked so much like her.

"Git ye back."

Clantail did not move. Melville dug her toes into Pechka's ribs and rolled her over. It happened so fast, Pechka couldn't even be startled when a pain worse than hitting the ground shot from her fingertips to her brain. Melville's heel was crushing Pechka's right index finger, bending it much farther than it should go. Tears welled in Pechka's eyes.

"Git ye back." Melville lifted her heel and next destroyed Pechka's middle finger on the same hand. Pechka clenched her teeth.

"Git ye back."

Then her ring finger. Unable to bear it, Pechka cried out. Pain and fear controlled her body. She felt the retreating hoofbeats through the earth. Clantail was ceding to Melville's demand and backing away. Not long after that, another set of footsteps approached.

"What is going on here?" It was Rionetta. She sounded so nonchalant. Pechka raised her head. Rionetta's expression was casual, too. She looked strangely lopsided without her right sleeve, which had been missing since before the last maintenance period. "Well, you needn't explain for me to grasp *this* situation."

"Oh? Will ye be 'elpin' me again?"

"The payment?" Rionetta asked.

"Same as 'en."

"But the situation is different now. The threat to you is much greater now, isn't it?"

"A shrewd imp, 'is one. Double?"

"Good-bye, then."

"Hold on!" Clantail's roar cut Rionetta and Melville's conversation off. "What are you talking about?!"

As if she were taking a stroll, Rionetta stepped forward and gave Clantail, nailed to the spot as per Melville's orders, a sidelong glance. "You speak as if I'm the peculiar one here. But isn't it rather that all of you were simply oblivious? For ten billion yen, one would expect someone to die, don't you suppose?"

"What...?!"

"'Twas bound t'come fer such terr'bly straenge creatures as magical gerls."

Rionetta stopped in front of Pechka.

"Cranb'ry told me b'fore. She recounted t'me tha' Akane be tryin' to slay Cranb'ry in th'ospital, tha' @Meow-Meow still be recallin' sommo' th'past after her mem'ries were chaenged, an' tha' Rionetta be mad for coin. She'll do aught fer a price. Like Ah jussaid."

Lazuline had always translated for Melville, but she wasn't there now, so Pechka could only understand parts of what she was saying.

Cranberry had told Melville some things?

Like that Akane had tried to kill Cranberry in the hospital?

That @Meow-Meow had remembered a little, even after her memories were overwritten?

And that Rionetta was obsessed with money, and she'd do anything if she got paid?

"First threats," said Rionetta, "and now you're calling me money-obsessed? How vicious."

"Rionetta...you...!" Clantail began.

Rionetta turned toward Clantail with a shrug. "I am not the only self-interested individual among us." After another half turn, she grinned at Pechka. The claws shot out of her right hand, glinting bright in the overwhelming light of the sun, and swung for Melville's neck. Melville raised her javelin to block the attack. The sound of metal clashing against metal and the harsh groaning of the javelin reached Pechka's ears.

"Wha' be this?" asked Melville.

"I can't condone injuring Pechka's hands. I made a promise. And besides, if I kill you, the game will be over, isn't that right? I shan't accept any requests from the Evil King." This time, Rionetta lashed out with the claws on her left hand, and Melville grabbed her upper arm to block that strike as well.

"Stae ye back." Melville wasn't saying that to Pechka or Rionetta. That order was for Clantail. Gripping Rionetta's left arm and blocking the right claw with her javelin, Melville kicked up at Rionetta's jaw with her free leg.

Well, that was only a guess on Pechka's part, though, once she had witnessed the result. She hadn't even seen what Melville had done. She could hear something ripping through the air with an explosive sound, followed by the heavy smack of a hard object colliding with something even harder, and afterwards, Melville was no longer standing on both legs; one was casually raised in the air. After having withstood soccer kicks from a demon, that one blow shattered Rionetta's head into countless wooden shards and tore her bonnet off into rags.

"Ah'll warn ye again. Stae ye back." Melville never took her eye off Clantail.

Rionetta's body slumped against Melville like a doll whose strings had been cut. Both arms dangled limp—until they wrapped around Melville's arms and squeezed. "Did you believe a puppet master...would leave her own body exposed?"

Rionetta's back split open, and something jumped out. It was a tiny girl who looked just like Rionetta as a human, except one size smaller, and she gripped a knife in her right hand. Melville's arms were bound. The girl kicked off Rionetta's back and leaped to thrust her knife into Melville's face. "My magic is puppetry. Mistaking a doll for my real body has brought about your demise." She stabbed Melville right between the eyes, jamming the knife all the way in until only the hilt was visible.

Melville's expression froze in shock, blood pouring down her face and dripping onto the ground. "Fine work," she said, before forcing her way out of the doll's grip. Knife still in her forehead, Melville grabbed the girl's arm with her right hand, her left going for the girl's neck.

A gasp of pain escaped from the girl. "H...ow...?"

Melville didn't reply. Her hand squeezed the girl's neck even harder. Pechka heard bones break as blood dribbled from the girl's mouth, and she just watched, unable to look away. The girl's face twisted in regret, and the wooden body slumped against Melville slid down and hit the ground on its front in a cloud of dust. With the knife still jutting from her head, Melville wrenched the girl's neck, then tossed her aside.

"But yer trick'ry be fer naught once ye've revealed the trick." Melville's body blurred, then changed shape. The knife that should have been stuck into her forehead was now in her right cheek. She yanked the blade out, and blood gushed from the wound. Tossing the knife away, Melville grabbed Pechka's collar again, roughly picked her up, and ran off.

"Ah must needs go. Meddlers be comin'."

☆ Nokko

Nokko's party had started at the Evil King's castle, so now they were running to the wasteland area to meet up with the others.

Nokko was pushing herself to sprint as fast as she possibly could, but at that pace, Lazuline had enough breath left to chatter. Of course, since Pfle was on Shadow Gale's back, she wasn't huffing or puffing, either. Glancing at Shadow Gale out of the corner of her eye, Nokko noticed she seemed pale. Was it because she was having a hard time running, or because their restored memories were upsetting her? Nokko didn't know.

As they relentlessly raced over the marble floors of the castle, the thuds of three sets of footsteps echoed and faded behind them.

"So is Melvy really the culprit, then?" said Lazuline. "But Bell was in Melvy's party, and Cherny, too. It just doesn't make sense for Melvy to have killed 'em."

"Think back on her appearance, though," said Pfle. "Who does she remind you of?" Who did Melville resemble? Pfle answered that question herself. "Yes—the Musician of the Forest, Cranberry. They look so alike. Of course, it's not simply a matter of looks. Melville is the only one I could consider to be the culprit—the Evil King lurking among the players." Pfle seemed more on edge than she'd been before the maintenance period. Maybe her restored memories were torturing her, too. "Melville is the one who stole Masked Wonder's coin, and also the one who manipulated Cherna Mouse's candy values. Her magic makes both of those feats possible."

"But Melvy's magic changes the color of her body to blend into the background, right? How could she do those things with that power?"

They passed through the gate into the wasteland area. The sound under them went from striking stone to stomping earth, and thick dust billowed up behind them. They had nearly reached Pechka's location.

"She underreported the scope of her powers," Pfle explained. "She told us her abilities were more limited than they really were in order to avoid exposing the crimes she committed with them. I'm positive that her magic includes not only the ability to freely alter her own appearance, but the appearance of anything. If so, she could falsify the display of her own magical phone by using her magic on it. She could make it look as if she didn't have the Miracle Coin, even though she actually did. And she did the same with Cherna Mouse's candy. All she had to do was make her phone's screen display a different number from what she actually held. And Cherna Mouse would have let Melville touch her phone without any suspicion."

"Are ya bein' serious?" asked Lazuline.

"I'm being serious. I believe that Melville is behind the incident where Genopsyko took @Meow-Meow down with her as well—or at the very least, I believe she may have masterminded it."

"You're just tryin' to blame everythin' on Melvy now, ain't ya?"

"Of all of us, Melville would have been the only one capable of hiding Genopsyko immediately when she was killed. She would have taken advantage of the confusion to camouflage the corpse and hide it. Then she'd simply have to retrieve it afterward."

"But Genopsyko was still alive after that! Me and Cherny both saw her in the wasteland town, and when we fought the Great Dragon, too."

"She didn't speak with anyone after Akane cut her up, and that's inexplicable. That would make no sense at all, if Genopsyko were acting under her own free will. But Genopsyko's actions *do* make sense if you assume they were induced by someone else's magic—Melville's accomplice."

"Someone was helping Melville?"

"There's a magic that can control marble statues. Such a skill could certainly control a corpse, as well," said Pfle.

Manipulating a corpse with magic. Just imagining it sent violent shivers down Nokko's spine.

"Ya mean Rionetta?" Lazuline doggedly opposed Pfle's argument. She was not convinced. "Maybe Melvy did do a bunch of bad stuff, worst case, but there's no reason for Rionetta to help her with all that! No way!"

"Well, I suppose you'd have to ask one of them directly. And even if Rionetta weren't proactively cooperating with Melville, I can think of a variety of ways Melville could have negotiated with her, such as bribery, threats, or intimidation. It was absolutely doable for her. And since all this fits so well, that makes it quite likely."

"Hnghh..." Lips pursed, Lazuline groaned. She didn't seem satisfied with that. "It's just... It's still weird. Melvy had no reason to kill Cherny. Cherny really took to her, and Melvy... I don't wanna say it like this, but she sure knew how to use her."

"If Melville is connected to Cranberry, then I'd wager that essentially, she requires no reason at all to kill anyone. If she told us she did it simply because she wanted to, my only response would be 'Oh, really?'"

"Hold on a sec. Sorry this is kinda basic, but...you been on about Cranberry this, Cranberry that. Who is this person? Ya said she looks like Melvy?"

Pfle was startled. It was so unusual for her to let surprise, upset, or any other emotions show on the surface. Shadow Gale turned around to look at her. The tension was obvious in not only her expression but even her neck, and she was clearly nervous. Nokko was surprised, too.

"Huh? What's up?" The look on Lazuline's face said she didn't know what all the shock was about. She tilted her head a bit.

Pfle raised her eyebrows slightly, as if in an attempt to cover up her surprise, and then her gaze shifted over to Nokko. "What about you, Nokko? Do you know Musician of the Forest, Cranberry?"

"Yes." Nokko nodded. She knew that name so well, it hurt: Cranberry, the Musician of the Forest, the magical girl who had forced her into a battle to the death to pass her magical-girl selection exam.

"Well, let's discuss that later," said Pfle. "Right now, we have something more important to deal with."

☆ Pechka

Pechka's broken fingers hurt so much, she thought she'd lose her mind. She'd have rather just gone crazy already, anyway. Her nails were broken, and her fingers were pointing in all different directions. The worst of them had broken bones poking through the bleeding muscle and skin. Pechka averted her eyes from her right hand. The sight of it made her feel faint.

But closing her eyes only recalled the images from just moments ago. On the dark interior of her eyelids, she saw Rionetta, neck broken, dangling limply from Melville's hand.

Rionetta had tried to save Pechka. She had apparently been cooperating with Melville for money, but she'd tried to save her teammate, anyway.

But Pechka had frozen. Right when Melville had been about to kill Rionetta, Pechka could have at least grabbed at Melville's legs. But she'd stayed still. She'd been frightened, terrified, and incapable of reaching out, even though she had returned to the game telling herself that she didn't want to be so passive and helpless anymore. But she still hadn't been able to do anything. It wasn't that she'd tried and failed. The failure had come before the attempt. She hadn't been able to move—despite the fact that Rionetta might have survived if Pechka had only done something. But Pechka had put herself first and frozen up. Just like last time.

What must Rionetta have felt when she'd tried to save Pechka? She'd always complimented Pechka's cooking, going on about how amazing it was. She'd had a sharp tongue, constantly fought with Nonako, and seemed scary to Pechka from the moment they met, but still, she had been a friend.

All these things kept whirling and whirling around inside Pechka's head. Meanwhile, Melville was running, carrying Pechka. She'd reached the edge of the wasteland area, and from that point, she began running in a clockwise circle. Clantail was chasing her. When she got too close, Melville would hurt Pechka to warn her off. Clantail kept about twenty yards back, following them at a distance neither too near nor too far. Between the clouds of dust, Pechka could see her teammate's face.

She seemed sad. Angry, too. Either way, it was the first time Pechka had ever seen her with such an expression.

Clantail's emotions never showed themselves on her face. Her gestures were what revealed the things she tried to keep hidden inside. When her deer tail whipped up after defeating an enemy, she was triumphant. When it wagged up and down during a meal, that meant she was enjoying it. When she didn't like it, she would rub her front legs against her stomach.

Right now, she was making no gestures that suggested what was going on inside her. There was only her face. She was trying to save Pechka. Clantail wanted to save her but couldn't even get close. Since she was fast, it would have been easy for her to catch up to Melville, but she was concerned for Pechka's safety and so was forced to keep her distance. Clantail had been the strongest in their party. She'd defeated the most monsters, she'd been entrusted with the Dragon-Killer back during the fight with the Great Dragon, and she'd also received +10 equipment from the Evil King's castle. Rionetta and Nonako had both counted on her to be their cornerstone in battle, and Pechka had relied on her most of all.

If Clantail could just catch up, then she'd be sure to win. Melville was very strong—she had fought Rionetta—but Clantail would certainly come out victorious.

If I could just slow Melville down somehow... But as the thought crossed Pechka's mind, agony shot through her right arm, and she screamed. Melville had smacked Pechka's left hand with her bow. Even though the blow was only a slap, Melville's strength was atypical, and her longbow, sturdy enough to withstand a magical girl's strength, was abnormally hard. It split the skin on her left hand, and the flesh underneath swelled out as blood poured from the wound. Pechka could see her own bones.

"Dinnae move."

That alone was enough to stop Pechka in her tracks. Her left arm hurt. She was scared. She knew that Clantail was being forced back because of her, but she still couldn't move. Her body was frozen.

"Ah'll finish 'is afore ye can 'inder me." Still racing at high speed, Melville flung Pechka ahead of her. Pechka didn't even have time to be startled before she hit the ground. She covered her face with her hands, but both of them were horribly mangled. She writhed in pain as the momentum from the throw sent her tumbling along the ground, and right when she came to a halt, Melville caught up to her. Melville stepped on Pechka's neck to hold her down and turned around to face Clantail.

"Stae ye back."

Clantail couldn't come close. Melville's foot was on Pechka's neck. One hard lean would break her neck—and Melville knew it. That put her in a position to tell Clantail what to do. Pechka understood that as well, but she still couldn't move.

Pechka's neck creaked under the strain. Melville was putting her weight on it. "Ye stae as ye be now. Dinnae move ye."

Melville nocked a javelin in her bow. She pulled back the bowstring, aiming for Clantail. Clantail flinched, but there was nowhere for her to run. Melville fired, and the shot ricocheted off Clantail's shield and into a high-rise building a few hundred yards behind her. It blasted the upper part of the building right off. The impact was more than Clantail could take, and she transformed her lower body into an alligator to brace herself as she was thrown back.

"Ah, th'plus ten Shield, eh? 'Tis staerdy indeed." Melville's second and third shots bounced off Clantail's shield, and each one blasted Clantail backward. The javelins kicked up dirt and sand wherever they landed, almost like explosions.

Clantail blocked them all with her shield. She wasn't getting hit—but she was hiding behind her shield, shoulders heaving. She had the +10 equipment, but Melville's bow was abnormally powerful and wielded by an abnormally powerful archer, as well. Pechka had seen Melville firing javelins many times, yet she had never seen Melville fire with such power and speed, plus modifier or not.

—Melville had been hiding it.

She'd been concealing her true ability. But for what? Had she anticipated that they would start killing one another?

Melville nocked another javelin in her bow. Pechka didn't know

if Clantail could take one more shot. And even if she did somehow manage to, what about the next one? And the one after that?

If Pechka acted, Clantail wouldn't have to just stand there and take it. She could get closer and strike back. But that would mean that Pechka, the hostage, would have to go. Pechka would die.

Pechka's arms and legs refused to move. They just wouldn't budge, no matter what. She couldn't breathe. But even if she couldn't move her limbs, she could move something else, at least, some other part—

"Wait!" Pechka yelled, and then she shuddered at what she'd done.

"What?" Melville leaned on her leg. The joints in Pechka's neck groaned.

"A magical girl…"

The weight on her neck lessened.

"A magical girl wouldn't fight this way."

Pechka knew she was provoking Melville. This might get her killed. It would be strange if Melville *didn't* kill her. Though Pechka had thought she'd come here ready to die, the idea made her teeth chatter. It felt like she was being teased, on the edge of having her internal organs crushed. Her heart was preparing for death, but her body couldn't catch up. Her body was crying, *I'm scared, I'm scared.*

"Talk." Melville didn't take her eyes off Clantail, but her attention was on Pechka. She was curious about what she had to say. Pechka shivered with cold despite the glaring wasteland sun overhead.

Pechka explained. Magical girls were strong. Strong and proud. That was something that Cranberry had aspired to. She had wanted magical girls to be tough, and that was why she had forced them into those killing matches. What the world needed was not cowardly magical girls who would take hostages to bully their opponents, but the kind who fought fair and square and defeated their foes without an advantage.

Pechka herself didn't even really understand what she was

saying as she went on. Her right hand hurt. So did her left. The weight holding down her neck pressed her face into the ground. She was scared. She was terrified. She felt like her heart was going to stop. She'd been grabbed by the collar and treated like an object, and she'd vomited up the acid in her stomach. Now all she could do was move her mouth as spit flew from it in an unsightly fashion. But still, her mouth was indeed moving.

A magical girl didn't need hostages. She wouldn't be running around like this. She wouldn't manipulate candy stores to get rid of someone. She didn't buy allies with money. A magical girl fought the strong fair and square. "If you fought each other as magical girls, fair and square…someone like you could never beat Clantail."

Melville smiled. "Ah nae be like Cranb'ry."

Pechka trembled. Melville was just like Cranberry in every way, and that smile—the first smile she'd shown Pechka—was just like Cranberry's, too. But Melville was saying she was different.

"Vict'ry be th'goal. Th'last un standin' be th'victor."

Pechka focused on her palms. She felt faint with pain.

She had to stay conscious. No matter if she was frightened and scared, if she just lay here trembling, she'd be killed anyway. She had to act. Even if she was terrified, even if she was panicking, even if all her limbs were paralyzed, there was still one thing she could do.

As a magical girl, Pechka had only ever been protected by others. In order to keep Pechka safe, her friend had let her cheekbones be broken, her jaw be smashed, her face become so swollen she couldn't see in front of her, but she'd still stood up to Cranberry until the Evil King had straddled her and punched her to death. But all Pechka had done was tremble. If she had done something, they might have been able to win, but her limbs had frozen up.

Then, after it had all ended, Cranberry and Fav had started talking as if Pechka weren't even there. "Nobody passed last time, or the time before that, or the time before that, either, hmm?" said Cranberry.

"If we don't pass someone this time, we're sure to get complaints, pon."

"I hate to pass this girl, since she barely fought at all. But we could say it's in light of her friend's grit."

"Mm-hmm, Cranberry, you've really matured, pon."

"Compliments won't get you anywhere."

When Cranberry, red with blood splatter, had casually announced that Pechka had passed, Pechka had sunk to the ground in relief. The tears didn't come until long after that. She'd even felt thankful to Cranberry, the girl who'd hit and hit and hit her friend right before her eyes to her brutal death. Pechka hadn't even considered her friend who was lying dead right there.

Why hadn't she been able to move? Why hadn't she done anything? She wanted to yell at herself for being grateful to Cranberry for sparing her life, to yell at herself for forgetting her friend in her relief.

Pechka had sworn to herself that it would never happen again. But she was still scared, shaking, paralyzed, tears and snot dripping from her face. She was hurt, terrified, convinced she was going to die.

—But, but, but, but, but…!

Even if she couldn't move her arms or her legs, there was still one thing that she could do.

Pechka activated her magic.

She'd dragged her speech out for five minutes, and her hands had stayed on the ground. To explain Pechka's magic in detail: She could transform anything she touched continuously for five minutes into the food of her choice. She would fill a pot with earth and then place her hands on it to turn it into food. This time, she was touching the ground directly.

In an instant, all the ground within fifteen feet of both of them was transformed into cold pumpkin and shrimp soup, and Pechka and Melville were right in the middle. Melville, from her standing position, and Pechka, lying down, were both drawn in by gravity, sinking into the sea. Pechka's hat floated up off her head and onto the surface.

Pechka was submerged in soup. She gulped down a mouthful. It was delicious and nutritious, the cooking everyone had told her they loved. Energy welled from inside her.

—Move! Move! Mooooove!

Pechka clung to Melville's leg. She couldn't use her hands or her fingers, so she hugged Melville's leg with her arms. Before Melville could kick Pechka off with her struggling, the sea of cold soup ended. With a pop, Melville and Pechka fell down into a big empty space, together with the cold soup. There were rock ledges green with moss, and lines of stalagmites. This place was familiar.

This time, they landed in real water. All the bubbles blinded Pechka. It was cold. She landed so hard, it felt like her arms would rip off. Desperately, she clung on.

They were in the underground lake. The path from the underground lake that connected the subterranean area to the stairs up to the library was right underneath the wasteland area. Pechka hadn't accounted for this. It was unexpected for her, but Melville was stunned, too. Pechka wouldn't let go. Finally, Melville kicked Pechka in the face. The water dulled its force, and Melville was a little frantic, too. The kick wasn't so bad. Even Pechka could handle it. Melville kicked at her again, but Pechka twisted to avoid it and kept clinging with her arms. Melville's third kick hit her in the shoulder. She could still handle it.

Large bubbles burbled up from Melville's mouth.

—A little longer! Just a little longer!

Melville's face twisted. She raised her javelin up and swung it down.

Pechka looked at the spear piercing her just above her navel. Red mingled with the orange of the soup, flowing out into the water. Her arms slackened. Melville slipped out and away from Pechka's grasp.

I was so close. Frustration welled up inside her, then quickly disappeared.

☆ Shadow Gale

Shadow Gale was running for where they were to meet Pechka. She still hadn't made sense of everything in her head.

She was sort of listening to Pfle's explanation. Unlike Lazuline, she wasn't going to ask questions about what the hell was going on. And she didn't care much about Pfle's explanation, since she'd heard it already. But more to the point, she just wasn't thinking straight. Her arms and legs were moving automatically, pumping as hard as they could.

She was in the lead with Pfle on her back as she raced along, unconcerned about their pace, passing by crumbling building after identical crumbling building as they headed for the meeting point.

Part of her was relieved by the explanation that Melville was the culprit—that in other words, she was the Evil King. Another part of her felt uneasy. *Is that really it?*

Why was she relieved? Because she'd suspected someone else might be the Evil King… She didn't want her to be the one, but there was one magical girl that had made her suspect that if there *was* an Evil King, it might be her. This was part of the reason for her unease.

Pfle's explanation was convincing. Melville's costume so closely resembled that of Musician of the Forest, Cranberry, that she wouldn't be able to talk her way out of it. It made the most sense for Melville to be the Evil King.

But Shadow Gale still couldn't relax. Pfle felt heavier on her back than usual. She had never felt this heavy before, not until their memories of Cranberry's exam had been restored. Pfle had been a very active participant back then. It had even seemed as if she'd been proactively cooperating with Cranberry. Until Shadow Gale had recalled what Pfle had been—

"Mamori!"

Shadow Gale was startled. She remembered what she was doing and stopped where she was, looking around and wondering what had happened. She was in the same old wasteland, and aside from Pfle on her back, there was nothing nearby…

Nothing?

"Where are Lazuline and Nokko?" Shadow Gale asked.

"I stopped hearing Lazuline's footsteps first, and after that, Nokko's vanished, as well. Lazuline disappeared instantly. I'd wager she used her magic. Nokko's sounded as if she ran off somewhere. By the time I looked back, she had already vanished, so I think she might have gone into one of the dilapidated buildings on the way."

"Why didn't you tell me immediately?!"

"I did. You were ignoring me."

Shadow Gale bit her lip. She hadn't noticed at all until Pfle had yelled at her. "So what do we do?"

"We're close to the meet-up point. Let's go there first. Our priority is making sure we can build a large group." Pfle was rational and selfish. She put her own safety first. Though Shadow Gale thought her suggestion had to be the right thing to do, the weight on Shadow Gale's back felt just a little heavier.

As Pfle had said, it wasn't long before they arrived at their goal. But Pechka wasn't where she was supposed to be.

"What..."

Instead, there was a magical phone, the wreckage of a doll that looked like Rionetta, and a tiny girl lying still on the ground. When Shadow Gale lifted her in her arms, her head dangled. She was already dead. There was no point in using any recovery medicine now.

Shadow Gale gently closed the girl's eyes. Her face looked like Rionetta's.

"Well, then," said Pfle. "What do you suppose happened?"

"...Looks like there was a fight." Shadow Gale turned around to find nothing. No one was there. High-rise buildings dotted the wasteland, stretching into the horizon. Scanning left to right, checking ahead and back, she saw it was all the same.

"From this point, we split up." Pfle pulled out her magical phone, summoned her carpet, and slid down from Shadow Gale's back onto it. She prompted Shadow Gale to pull out her phone, too. "You're registered as part of our party, now. You should be able to tell where Nokko is, right? Go and search for her."

"What do we do about Lazuline?"

Pfle's eyes were on the screen of her own magical phone. She had the map application activated and was checking her party members' current positions. Pfle's icon was right here, Nokko was a little ways away, and Lazuline's icon was nowhere to be found. "Lazuline isn't in the wasteland, at least. Leave her be."

"And you, miss?"

"The others are probably fighting Melville. I'll head over to back them up. We must defeat Melville, or none of us have any hope."

"Then is this really the time to be looking for Nokko?"

"Do you think there's a reason she left us?"

Why had Nokko had left Shadow Gale and Pfle just now? Shadow considered it, but couldn't think of anything.

"That's another serious cause for concern," said Pfle. "There's some risk in splitting up, but our numbers are limited, so we have no choice. If you feel you're in even the slightest danger, flee immediately. Don't forget: If you sense danger, run."

☆ Melville

She had underestimated Pechka.

For Pechka's magic to work, she had to be touching her target with her palms, and she also required five minutes to prepare, so her powers weren't usable in battle. Melville had figured as long as she wasn't foolish enough to let Pechka lay her hands on her for five minutes straight, her magic would be useless. She hadn't imagined that Pechka would be capable of such a wide area of effect.

But no matter. It had been Melville's fault for giving her five minutes to spare at all, forgetting about her magic, and letting Pechka talk freely so that Melville could show off how unconcerned she was. She had been upset when the differences between her and Cranberry had come up, and she'd done a poor job of hiding it. If not for that, she never would've considered allowing all of Pechka's awkward babble.

* * *

The beautiful Musician of the Forest had swooped down before Melville as she was hunting animals in the hills and fields with her handmade bow and arrows. Even the great bear, the god of the mountain, had been no match for her. She had admired the Musician of the Forest so much, yearned so badly to be like her, that her magical-girl form looked just like the person she adored.

Melville had admired Cranberry—worshiped her. But despite that, she'd chosen a different path from her idol. No, she'd been *forced* to choose a different path.

Melville's magic was the power to change the surface colors of any object. She could erase what was supposed to be there and create something else. Her powerful ability could deceive her enemies' eyes, confuse them, and whittle down their strength. Melville's style was to mislead and trick her enemies, then shoot them down.

But her magic didn't work on Cranberry at all. Even though Melville had learned to move almost soundlessly, Cranberry's hearing was sharper than her sight. She could sense the heartbeat of any living creature. If an object wasn't alive, then she could send out sonar-like waves to pinpoint its location. Magic that could only change appearances didn't mean much to Cranberry.

Cranberry's identity was founded on her own strength. But Melville's core principle was that, since she couldn't be as good as Cranberry, she would do things a different way.

She schemed. She deceived. She used surprise attacks and assassination. Temporary alliances. Money, too. As long as she could win, that was enough. The strongest of all was the last one standing.

But Melville never got over it. After all her training and battles, she was no longer a rookie. But even as she was getting closer to Cranberry, she felt more and more like she would never catch up.

The strong rule in the mountains. Magical girls were the strongest and greatest of all. The strongest of them would truly be the greatest.

Melville had been chosen as a magical girl through Cranberry's exam, and afterward, she would cooperate with Cranberry when needed. Unlike the other magical girls, her memory had never been erased. It had been Melville's wish that she retain her memories, and Cranberry had granted it.

Melville wanted to be able to beat Cranberry, one day. With that desire in mind, she had continued on as a magical girl until she hit a wall she could never overcome. Then, while she was busy struggling, Cranberry, the one who was supposed to have been the strongest of them all, had been killed. When Cranberry's deeds were exposed, the authorities had caught Melville, too. Before she was even over the shock of Cranberry's death, her qualifications as a magical girl had been stripped from her, and she was back to being only a girl.

Then this game had begun. Someone had returned her powers to her. She had regained her identity as admirer of the Musician of the Forest, Cranberry; her strength; and her way of living. Scanning the other participants, she'd noticed a number of familiar faces. They were the victors Melville had seen before when she'd helped Cranberry with her exams. Some were examinees whose names had been written in the records Fav had left behind. There were also a number of new faces there as well, but Melville was certain they were all victors of Cranberry's exams.

Someone had gathered all these girls who'd passed and forced them to play a game. In other words, this meant Cranberry was alive, right? No one but Cranberry would have done something like this. Either her death had been a lie, or she had faked it herself. Cranberry was so strong, there was no way she could have died, Melville had thought with joy.

The other girls had seemed to think this game was exactly what it seemed. No surprise there. They'd all forgotten. But Cranberry would never make them play a game that was entirely safe and secure. They'd been told that they should cooperate to defeat the Evil King, but Cranberry, of course, would have wanted them to do something else. She had gathered the victors here to make them play, so as to select the true victor from them all. Of course, Melville had to be the winner.

Melville pretended to be a regular participant while she went around killing the other players in secret.

If she'd fought Masked Wonder head-on, the other girl would have been a great challenge. Seeing her face off with Cherna Mouse had been enough evidence of that. She wasn't an opponent to fight head-to-head. It was best to take her by surprise.

Melville had been glad when Akane had taken herself out of the running. In the hospital, Akane had been seething with hatred for Cranberry and apparently still remembered bits and pieces. She'd gone around saying, *Musician, musician*, at every opportunity, so Melville had been worried she might cause one of the others to remember.

Speaking of dropouts, Genopsyko and Magical Daisy were responsible for their own deaths, too. Both Genopsyko, who could nullify any attack, and Magical Daisy, who was very experienced and used powerful one-hit KO magic, were troublesome enemies. The removal of those two had been a big help to Melville.

Cherna had been manageable and easy to control. By using her to monopolize hunting grounds, Melville had sown the seeds of discord between the parties and slowed down the exchange of information. She had considered using Cherna up until the end…but when she saw Cherna crush Pfle's tank, she changed her mind. If Cherna had turned on her at any point, it would have been too much for Melville to handle.

@Meow-Meow. It had seemed as if her memories were beginning to return, perhaps triggered by the things Akane had said. Though she had genuine strength even without her memories, and was able to battle it out with Akane and win. Melville had used Genopsyko's body to finish her off. @Meow-Meow had felt strongly for her allies, so to kill her, Melville was forced to use those allies to lower her guard. Melville had let them get a glimpse of Genopsyko beforehand and left the warning message that there was a traitor. She'd also created a wound on the face of the fake Genopsyko, then later, when she had made Rionetta control Genopsyko's body, Melville had erased the injury, suggesting that Genopsyko had survived and that @Meow-Meow was the traitor.

Melville had used Rionetta because she had seen her exam in full, and she knew how Rionetta made her living. She was basically an assassin who only worked for money. Of course, Rionetta couldn't let the Magical Kingdom know about that. Melville had sneaked into Rionetta's house to leave three million yen in cash on her table. When the game had started up again, Melville had revealed that she'd been the one who gave it to her, adding that she hoped it would help repay Rionetta's father's debts. Melville had lured her with money while also implicitly threatening her—she knew where Rionetta lived and about her family. That was how she had used Rionetta to eliminate @Meow-Meow.

As for the remaining magical girls… There was Pfle. She was all talk, and she'd lost her wheelchair, too. Shadow Gale. If that ten-legged tank was the best she could do, then no problem there. Nonako Miyokata. It depended on the monsters available, but Melville could kill her, even two-on-one against her dragon. Detec Bell. Not only was her magic unsuited for battle, she could hardly use it at all in the game. Pechka. Out of the question.

The only tough one would be Lazuline. The previous Lapis Lazuline had been one of the top veterans among the victorious survivors of Cranberry's exams. She'd been a shrewd old hag, and even before becoming a magical girl, she'd never let her guard down for a second in her life. Since the old Lazuline had picked her out, the current Lapis Lazuline would be no weakling, and her keen intuition would be a threat to Melville, too. How to eliminate her…?

That was the point when all the players' memories had returned and Melville had lost her advantage. If she had only managed to kill Detec Bell instantly and steal her phone…but it was too late for that.

Now that it was all out in the open, Melville couldn't hide herself among the players anymore. Her appearance had been born from her desire to be just like Cranberry. Her vines, roses, and pointed ears were already the same. She probably wouldn't be targeted immediately based purely on her resemblance, but they would certainly be very suspicious of her. She couldn't stay hidden any longer.

* * *

Melville had made a mistake in underestimating Pechka and paid for it dearly, but that didn't make this an instant game over. Melville stabbed Pechka with her javelin and finally slipped away when the other girl's grip loosened. She made herself invisible and escaped, and immediately afterward, she heard something hit the lake, along with a spray of water.

It was Clantail. She'd come in through the hole Pechka had made, her lower body a fish…no, a dolphin. She kicked through the water with her large tail, straight for Pechka.

Melville ignored Clantail and swam for the shore, deftly erasing drips of water, her footprints, and herself as she went. Making it look as if nothing had ever been there, she circled the lake.

Clantail was using her magical phone. She had to be trying to heal her companion's injury. Pechka was alive, barely. Melville had made sure the stab wound wouldn't kill her immediately.

Still invisible, Melville moved around the lake's edge to come behind Clantail. With Pechka in her arms, she wasn't watching out for Melville. Her unguarded back made a very nice target.

If Melville used her bow, the sound of her pulling the string back might alert Clantail. Even if she was no Cranberry, all magical girls had keen senses, which of course included sharp hearing. And besides, no matter how big this cavern was, it was still an enclosed space. If she triggered a cave-in and got trapped in here, Melville would be helpless.

Now, she should use her javelin the proper way and throw it by hand. By the time Clantail noticed it flying toward her, she'd be impaled by the transparent steel. Slowly and soundlessly, Melville raised her weapon, then hurled it at Clantail's back.

☆ Pechka

When Pechka opened her eyes, she was in Clantail's arms. Following her memories back, she recalled being stabbed by a javelin, and she looked at her own stomach. There was a hole in her clothing, and the area around it was all red, but she wasn't in pain. There was no spear. She tried touching the spot and found no wound.

"What a relief..." Clantail was smiling. She seemed about to cry. Pechka was in her arms, so their faces were close.

Glancing at Clantail's lower body, Pechka saw it had transformed into a dolphin. *It's one of her cuter transformations. I'll classify that one together with the deer and the pony,* Pechka thought, her mind still hazy.

Just then...she suddenly got a whiff of something. The smell was exactly like the one hovering over them and on Pechka herself, and it was circling the lake. Pechka looked around, but she couldn't see anything that could be the source. Before Pechka even realized what was going on, she acted. She wrapped her arms around Clantail's shoulders and reversed their positions in the water.

A brutal impact hit her back. She felt like her body would be torn apart.

Pain. Heat. Cold. Agony. Fear.

She fell into the blackness together with all these negative feelings. But one single thing inside her shone beautifully. Pechka had finally been able to act. She had been able to protect her dear friend. Satisfied with this result, she silently closed her eyes.

Her friends were there, behind her eyelids. Her family, too. Nonako and Rionetta were fighting, and Clantail was trying to make them settle down. Ninomiya was there. That girl who was so much like him was there, too. They were all smiling. Pechka smiled. It was nice. This was fun, and she was glad.

☆ Melville

Pechka had gotten her yet again. Her javelin should have pierced Clantail's back, but Pechka had spun them around so that it hit her instead. Now Clantail was aware of her enemy, and before Melville could fire off a second javelin, she dived down into the water with Pechka.

Yes, it was Pechka again. Melville spat on a rock. She tried to calm herself, but she was so irate that she was ready to boil over with humiliation and rage.

Clantail hadn't noticed Melville, but Pechka had. She'd detected Melville's presence, sensed what she was doing, and blocked the spike Melville had thrown at Clantail's back. There had to be a reason why Pechka had been the only one to notice. Melville's movements had been entirely silent. No one could have sensed her, unless their hearing was as sharp as Cranberry's. The only thing besides sight and hearing was scent. Perhaps just as Cranberry's ability to control sound conferred upon her a powerful sense of hearing, Pechka's cooking abilities gave her an amazing sense of smell.

Coming up with an explanation for her failure enabled Melville to finally calm her heart. She took another lance in hand. No matter how many she threw, she would never run out.

The surface of the water was still. Clantail was still in her dive and didn't rise.

Was Pechka alive or dead? Melville had felt that hit. She was probably dead. What would Clantail do when her teammate died? She would attack, for sure. But Melville had concealed her presence, and Clantail had no way to find her.

Melville touched her hand to the bare rock face. She couldn't sense any movement within the water.

She figured she should run. Out in the wasteland, she'd be unbeatable. She would rather not fight underground, given the choice. There wasn't enough space. If she threw her javelin hard, she was bound to cause a cave-in, and then she'd be the one getting trapped and injured.

But running away now would allow the survivors to meet up. She would much rather take them out one by one. Whittling down the enemy's forces was clearly better than fighting them all at once.

Melville looked up at the roof. Pechka's magic had opened a large hole above them. And in her scuffle with Clantail, for the first time in the game, Melville had pulled the bowstring back as hard as she could. The rare items she'd acquired thanks to the Miracle Coin, the Power Talisman, and the Bow of the Evil God had enabled her to destroy one of the buildings and form a crater. That power was good, but that sort of dramatic destruction might have drawn attention from the other magical girls. It would be best if she could kill Clantail surreptitiously.

The surface of the water shifted and rippled. Melville focused. If she flung the javelin straight at Clantail's face, that would void half the point of going invisible. Raising up onto her tiptoes, she curved her spine. She'd mastered the art of moving silently in an attempt to catch up to Cranberry, but ultimately, that had not been enough to surpass Cranberry, either. But it had built the foundation of Melville's combat style.

Clantail's head floated to the surface twenty yards from the opposite shore. Her shoulders and torso emerged, and she was cradling Pechka. The girl was still in Clantail's embrace. Her limbs were loose and limp. Clantail's head was drooping, so Melville couldn't see her expression from where she was standing.

If she was holding Pechka, that meant her arms were occupied.

Circling around to Clantail's right side, Melville observed Pechka. Blood flowed from her back, staining Clantail. Her wound hadn't healed, and her face and arms were beyond pale. They were ashen. Melville had seen the same thing many, many times during Cranberry's exams. Pechka was dead.

With her lower body still in the water, Clantail was approaching the shore. It would be best to kill her before she left the water, since on the lake, her movement would be limited. Positioning herself at Clantail's right flank, Melville adjusted her grip on her javelin. About a hundred and thirty yards to her target. It was a good distance. She readied her javelin, and the instant before she threw, her eyes met Lazuline's— Lazuline?

A crushing sense of unease washed over Melville.

"Are ya really the Evil King, Melvy?" Lapis Lazuline was right beside Clantail. She was facing Melville and speaking to her—even though she had to be invisible. Her eyes were filled with pure anger, and her face was twisted in a glare. This was the first time Melville had ever seen Lazuline angry. Melville retreated half a step. She was overwhelmed.

Though only for a moment, she was confused. Melville's specialty was creating something from nothing. None of the other magical girls here could have done something like that.

Clantail's head turned to follow Lazuline's gaze—toward Melville. Lazuline threw a sparkling blue orb, teleported toward it and caught it, then threw it for another teleport while she was still in midair, and then she was standing right in front of Melville.

"Are ya seriously the Evil King, Melvy? Are you the one who killed Bell?" she asked, facing the invisible and silent Melville. Lazuline could tell where she was.

Melville took a deep lungful of moist underground lake air. If Lazuline was going to give her a moment, then she would use it to suppress her rising confusion, discomfiture, and shock.

Back when they had been exploring the Evil King's castle area, Lazuline had given Clantail a gem. Insurance, in case Lazuline was suddenly attacked up front. Had Clantail returned that gem to Lazuline? At the very least, Melville hadn't witnessed the exchange.

Clantail had dived into the water not only to avoid Melville's attack and attempt to heal Pechka—she had been sending a plea to Lazuline for help. Lazuline had responded and teleported to the gem in Clantail's possession.

The question that remained was how Lazuline knew where Melville was. Melville threw a javelin, which Lazuline dodged easily before making a beeline for her.

—Was it intuition? That was all?

Melville shot a look over to Clantail. She was already just about at the shore.

Clantail's magic was to transform her lower body into any nonhuman creature. That could be a mammal, reptile, amphibian, fish, or anything else. As long as it was alive, anything went. However, any creature that she transformed into would never have anything above the neck—because that was where Clantail's upper body would be growing.

Melville knew all about Clantail, since Melville had assisted Cranberry in her exam. Clantail had transformed into various animals then, but all of them had been only from the neck down. She had never transformed into an animal with a head.

An animal's sensory organs were generally situated above the neck. Some odd cases might have them on the legs or torso, but those creatures didn't have particularly potent senses. None of them would be good enough to detect Melville when she was moving silently. A snake's ability to sense heat, a dog's sense of smell, and a bat's sonar would all have been a threat to her, but Clantail would have needed the head of the animal to use those sensory organs. For that reason, Clantail's magic didn't pose a substantial threat to Melville. If she defeated Lazuline first, her chances of victory were good.

Clantail gently laid Pechka's body down on the shore. Lifting her head, she looked at Melville. With an expression more bestial than any animal, she glared.

"*Melviiiiiille!*" she howled, charging. Her lower body was a lion. She'd most likely not chosen a horse because she'd figured hooves would be dangerous here on the slippery rock, and she was soaked, too.

Clantail's approach was swift. Even if she couldn't see Melville, Clantail would know where she was because Lazuline was fighting her. She would be forced to fight two-on-one. After turning aside Lazuline's punch, Melville blocked a kick with her longbow. She had no time.

Melville changed all the colors of the rock surface around Clantail to a perfect black that reflected no light. Now Clantail wouldn't be able to see the irregularities of the ground, making it extremely difficult to run. Would she slow down, simply abandon herself to her anger and race full speed only to stumble—or would she hesitate momentarily? Melville just had to buy some time, no matter how brief. She would use those moments to kill Lazuline.

Melville swiped a jab away, then deflected each part of Lazuline's jab, hook, uppercut, straight combination with the back of her hand or palm. She tossed her longbow aside. In close quarters, it would only get in the way. She thrust the javelin in her right hand at Lazuline's feet, but Lazuline blocked the stab with the bottom of her foot. Melville couldn't sense that her invisibility put Lazuline at any disadvantage, even though she couldn't have seen either Melville or her javelin.

Lazuline had said her intuition had always been sharp, but the previous Lazuline had polished it. Melville couldn't help but think that the old Lazuline had anticipated a battle to the death against multiple opponents. Lazuline could dodge attacks from behind. She could sense attackers, even when taken by surprise. She could see through traps. And of course, she was a talented fighter, too.

One second had passed.

What had the previous Lazuline been thinking? That hag had been cunning and tenacious. What had she been thinking, training a magical girl who carried her name for a murderous battle, training her hard, while she retired carefree? She'd just been preparing a scapegoat for when something happened, hadn't she?

This girl, designed for a battle royal, had sharp fists. She was precise and never hesitated. She hit Melville's shoulder, grazed her cheek, and cut off a chunk of her hair, which floated away. Melville stopped trying to be silent. She let the sounds of her movement, her clothing, breathing, everything make noise. The two girls punched each other. Exchanged blows. Thrust, stumble back, spin, back fist, counter with an elbow. Melville hit Lazuline on the wrist to block but couldn't slow down the strike and got hit in the neck. Unflinching, Melville thrust out her javelin and skewered Lazuline's thigh, holding her in place to drive a heel into her right foot and break it.

Two seconds had passed.

Lazuline didn't cry out. She didn't even show a hint of pain. Without hesitation, she crushed a gem in her right hand and scattered the fragments. Before Melville could understand what she was doing, Lazuline had vanished, and Melville was taking a punch in the back. Her ribs cracked. It had hurt her kidney, too. Melville swung her javelin around to the rear, but Lazuline wasn't there. Melville raised her arm to block a hit aimed at her temple, but when she tried to strike back, Lazuline was already gone. After a hit to the torso, Melville staggered. She predicted the following attacks to her shoulder, arm, and thigh, so aside from the first shot, she somehow managed to avoid any major damage, but she couldn't manage to strike back. She was being kicked and punched from every direction, as if she were at the center of an angry mob. Lazuline was only one girl, but she seemed like a crowd.

The fragments of blue gem sparkled as they rained down. Each one of them was a deadly weapon. Lazuline teleported from shard to shard again and again, her afterimages layering over each other. She wasn't giving Melville the time to strike back.

Three seconds had passed.

Melville fell to the ground. Unable to withstand Lazuline's flurry of violence, she fell awkwardly on her back…or so she made it seem, but of course, that wasn't the truth. Pain or injury couldn't rob Melville of her will to fight. Everything she did was with victory in mind. Cowardly or dirty though it might have been, Melville had chosen a way of life that would never shame her to Cranberry.

By putting her back on the ground, Melville had eliminated her greatest blind spot. The solid cold of the rock surface seeped into her cracked ribs. Lazuline was sure to reveal herself in order to get one final hit on Melville, weakened and downed. That was when Melville would strike. But a single attack wouldn't be enough to win. If you considered her opponent's injuries and her own, her opponent's stance and her own, her opponent's abilities and her own, and the fact that the timing was up to Lazuline, they were even. There was no point in keeping things that way. What Melville needed was victory. To that end, she'd add just a bit of spice.

Four seconds had passed.

Lazuline revealed herself, and simultaneously, Melville did, too, and added color to her previously invisible body. She mixed up geometry, color, and shadow to create a deceptive image. Lazuline's foot thrust out, ready to stomp down on Melville on the ground.

Melville thrust her javelin out, crossing past Lazuline's leg to pierce unerringly through her ribs and her heart behind them. Lazuline looked down at her. Melville, awkwardly sprawled on her stomach, was reflected in her furious eyes.

When Melville had been invisible, Lazuline had been landing accurate hits. Suddenly seeing her, lying on her face, Lazuline had become just a bit bolder. In order to make her final strike to Melville's vitals, her forward lunge had been a little larger, and that had allowed Melville, who was actually lying on her back in wait, to connect with her javelin first.

If Melville had presented to her a completely fake image with no real body present, Lazuline would probably not have fallen for it. But Melville had only made it seem as if she were flipped over the other way, though she had actually been in that spot. Using herself as bait, she'd managed to create just the smallest opening in Lazuline's guard. Lazuline, her heart pierced, had landed her stomp, too, but it was weaker, and she had missed Melville's vitals.

Five seconds had passed.

Melville had made it. Clantail wasn't there yet.

Lazuline collapsed, and Melville stood to trade places with her. Immediately, she made herself invisible. Lazuline's defeat didn't mean this was over. Melville erased the blood splattered on Lazuline as well as her own blood, everything. All that she left visible was Lazuline herself. Once Clantail approached Lazuline to save her, Melville would have this in the bag. She would stab her with her javelin and end the fight.

A vibration in the rock surface. Clantail had launched herself into the air. She was leaping over the black ground.

Foolish. That made her an easy target.

Clantail was twenty yards away. Her lower body swelled, about to transform right there. But no matter what she tried to shape-shift into, she wouldn't make it in time. No animal could attack from so far away or close the distance faster than Melville's javelin. The lance would stab her first.

Clantail's swollen lower abdomen split. Tough, shining-red scales appeared, and she flung her forelegs out in front of her, each claw sharp and as large as a small human. Her tail was as thick as an oil drum, as long as multiple people lay head to foot. She extended a pair of wings massive enough for such a body. They flapped hard enough to make waves on the surface of the water.

Melville remembered. There was no way she could forget this. It was the Great Dragon.

Clasping her javelin, Melville's hand trembled. She couldn't steady her aim. She knew she should aim for the upper body, but Clantail was high above her, her great lower body concealing her human parts.

This wasn't a situation Melville could fight in. She should stay concealed and get out. The Great Dragon was so big, Melville couldn't expect to do much damage throwing javelins by hand. She just had to get some distance. A shot from her longbow, which could destroy buildings and blast craters into the earth, could pull it off.

When Melville tried to get away, something gently brushed her ankle. It was Lazuline's hand. She was still facedown on the ground in a pool of her own blood. She was dead. What Melville felt against her ankle was a dead person's hand. The body heat was bleeding out of her.

But she had moved. Was it out of obsession? Malice?

Before Melville could find out, the Great Dragon gave a horizontal swipe with its claws. It sliced Melville, still invisible, into chunks and flung them into the lake with a spurt of blood.

☆ Shadow Gale

After splitting with Pfle, her back felt strangely lighter.

She had zero intention of opposing Pfle's order to run immediately if she felt she was in danger. Shadow Gale moved forward slowly, observing closely for anything abnormal that might be even the slightest bit off.

Speaking of odd, Nokko's disappearance was bizarre, in and of itself. Nokko had been running at the tail end of their group, so she had to have seen Lazuline disappear. There was no reason for her to fail to mention Lazuline's absence and then silently withdraw from the line.

In Shadow Gale's left hand was the Dragon Shield, and in her right she held the +7 wrench. Ready to respond, no matter who attacked or from where, Shadow Gale was not running along the vast wasteland, but walking. Nokko's icon was close. There was a high-rise about a hundred yards ahead. It was near there.

Maintaining her pace and staying as alert as possible, Shadow Gale approached the high-rise, and then she was there. She touched the wall of the building. The texture was rough. It was just another dilapidated structure, nothing special about it. It was no different from the other countless decrepit edifices dotting the wasteland. It was just a game object.

She checked Nokko's position with her magical phone. It had not changed at all since Shadow Gale had first launched the map. Nokko was still there. Shadow Gale tucked her phone into her pocket and took her wrench in hand.

The party location function in the map app didn't indicate the person's location, but rather the location of their device. It was very possible to turn a magical phone into bait to lure her into a trap. Whether or not Nokko would do such a thing herself, it was also possible someone else would use her phone to that end.

Shadow Gale slid along the wall, circling around to the front of the building. She slowed down further, cautious, careful, inclining her ears to even the slightest sound, taking smooth steps.

It was silent. She noticed no sounds—but she did smell something. She remembered this. The final floor in the subterranean area, where all the magical girls had fought together, came back to her mind's eye. This was the smell of something burned and scorched.

When she reached the front of the building, Shadow Gale

peeked inside. There was a black lump there. It wasn't clear what it had once been. It was just a cinder the size of a human torso. The soot-black floor around it had to mean this thing had been burned up here.

Beside the lump, a magical phone lay on the ground. Something was attached to it. When she saw it, Shadow Gale immediately closed her eyes. She had been careful and cautious up until this point, but right when it counted most, she was closing her eyes. Was that because she wanted to unsee what she'd just witnessed, or was she just averting her eyes from reality?

A girl's severed hand clasped the magical phone tight. It was burned coal-black from the wrist halfway up the back. Only one of the players had a hand of that size. The image of that hand, still so small, was burned under Shadow Gale's eyelids, and shutting her eyes wasn't enough to erase it.

MASTER SIDE #10

"Hey. I've been waiting for you."

The new automatic door opened quietly and smoothly, inviting the guest in. The girl had designed it to do that. Though it was obvious and taken for granted that the door should slide quietly and without friction, the girl nodded in satisfaction.

The magical phone lying on the table activated, and an artificial voice cried, "Snow White!"

"Shut up. You're obnoxious." A snap of the girl's fingers, and the phone turned off.

The guest looked from left to right. She might have been concerned about the black screens on the abundance of monitors. Because of that, the room was dark, and the only source of light was the glow from beyond the frosted glass door.

The girl swept her arm across the table, knocking everything to the floor: The monitor, notebook, magical phone, pencil stand, and pen hit the ground with a poof of dust. The girl rose from her seat, spread her palms with a smile, and indicated a chair before the table. "Sit, sit," she said, ushering in her guest.

The magical girl in white—Snow White—took three steps forward from the entrance, pulled back the chair, and sat.

The girl snapped her fingers, and on top of the table appeared a porcelain saucer and cup, pure white like fresh snow, and the cup was filled with a liquid the color of young leaves. "You didn't touch the café au lait the other day, Snow White, so I tried making some green tea."

Snow White showed no gratitude for the girl's kindness and made no move to touch the drink.

The girl closed one eye. She seemed less offended and more amused. "The truth is, the game is juuust about over."

For the first time, Snow White's expression changed.

The girl studied her surprised guest and opened her closed eye. She then nodded a couple times and brought the tea to her mouth. "That's the truth, no jokes and no lies. Will the Evil King win, or the players? Only a little longer, and the game'll be over. Now we juuust need to see the results… I wonder what'll happen? What do you think'll happen?"

Snow White's expression had already evened out again. She didn't reveal her emotions.

The girl said, "It's surprisingly bitter," and placed the cup down on the saucer. "Of course, I'm not trying to say we should finish up these negotiations and please go home since the game is ending. I never wanted to negotiate with the Magical Kingdom in the first place. It'd be best if they would just change the system, but I know how many years it takes for them just to change *one* regulation."

The girl snapped her fingers again. The green liquid inside her cup turned black, bubbling, and fizzy. She lifted the cup to her lips. "I prefer this, after all," she said, face relaxing into a smile. "I don't plan to sit back and wait for that. I don't want things to take forever, and there's no way I'm gonna stand for bad magical girls running loose in the meantime. So I'm not gonna negotiate with the Magical Kingdom. I'm gonna ignore them and do what I want."

The girl raised her hand up to eye level. Dust gathered into a spiral at her fingertip and became shining particles that merged into a nine-by-nine cube puzzle with all-white squares. The cube floated on the girl's fingertip, changing without being touched, and on one side appeared an entirely empty square.

"This empty square is the game world, about to decide the victor." The girl grinned, and the expression made her glasses slide down. She supported them with her pointer finger. "Do you get what I'm trying to say? Inside this little tiny square space, I made a world and reproduced their data in there. I'm saying that's what I'm capable of."

Snow White listened to her without giving a response.

The girl continued. "Cranberry's little mascot left logs of her final exam. I hacked those logs from the Magical Kingdom. I have all the data of the magical girls who participated on hand."

Snow White twitched just very slightly.

"You get what I mean? I can reproduce La Pucelle, Hardgore Alice, and all the others inside my game. They'd be just as they were when they were alive, inherit all their old memories perfectly, like the originals. And I don't really know for sure, but I bet they'd probably have souls, too. I'd make them just for you, Snow White, and the storage space and tech requirements be damned."

The girl stood from her chair, put her hands on the desk, and leaned her face in close toward Snow White. There were less than four inches between them. The breath from the girl's nose stirred Snow White's bangs. "I wanted to negotiate with you, Snow White. Let's join forces. Let's change the world together. Let's create a world where righteous magical girls can live with pride."

CHAPTER 11
AND ET CETERA

☆ **Shadow Gale**

Shadow Gale and Pfle had moved over to the shop in the Evil King's castle area, and they were sticking firm to their spot. Shadow Gale was modifying a stun gun with her wrench and scissors, while Pfle was watching from her carpet.

Shadow Gale didn't think Pfle understood what was being done. Knowledge and skills wouldn't help you comprehend the principles behind magic-based modification. Pfle had to be pretending to watch Shadow Gale work while her mind was actually on something else.

The message from Pfle came immediately after Shadow Gale had discovered Nokko.

Meet up with me at the Evil King's castle. Hurry. Until we see each other, no further contact needed.

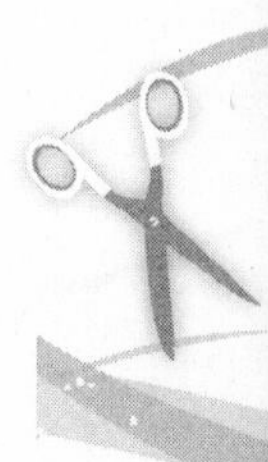

The message was brief. When Pfle sent brief messages, it meant they had to hurry. Shadow Gale retrieved Nokko's magical phone, but she was forced to leave her charred remains on the spot. She merely pressed her hands together before she left.

She never did find out who had killed Nokko. All that remained with her was the feeling that she had failed to protect her. It took all her strength to carry her heavy legs to the Evil King's castle, and before long, she was joined by Pfle.

Shadow Gale reported Nokko's death in a tight, strained voice.

On her magic carpet, Pfle asked, "Really?" to which Shadow Gale emphasized that there was no mistaking it. Pfle received that with an "Oh" and didn't reveal her thoughts on the matter.

Once they arrived at the shop terrace in the Evil King's castle, Pfle finally began sharing what she had witnessed.

Pfle had been going after Clantail and the others, following the trail of a chase and a fight. She'd passed the rubble of a building, a massive crater, and then a big hole in the ground. Immediately, Clantail had emerged from it. Pfle had hidden in the shadow of a high-rise to watch her.

Clantail's lower body had been transformed into a gecko, the same one as during the Great Dragon fight, most likely in order to climb up out of the hole. Pechka had been under her right arm, Lazuline her left, and she'd had a severed head tied to her waist. It was an extremely gruesome sight. Pfle said that Clantail had been completely soaked, dripping water on the ground.

"I was a ways away, but neither Pechka nor Lazuline seemed to be alive—they were both wounded and hadn't been healed. As for the severed head...I couldn't see the face from my position, but judging from the hair color and style, as well as the general circumstances, I'm almost certain it was Melville." In other words, Clantail, Lazuline, and Pechka had most likely clashed with Melville, and only Clantail had survived in the end, Pfle concluded.

Clantail had then turned her lower body into a horse and begun trudging toward town. Pfle had rushed toward the Evil

King's castle, she said, taking care to avoid Clantail's notice. "I believe she was headed to the wasteland town to bury their bodies. Now then, next."

Having finished sharing her information with Shadow Gale, Pfle pulled out her magical phone and pressed the HELP button. The wind blowing through the terrace teased her hair and fluttered the edges of her magic carpet. There wasn't anything out of the ordinary about it, and yet, something was strange.

A black-and-white hologram appeared above the screen. "What do you need, pon?"

Pfle asked, "Can I take it that the goal of this game has been to gather and punish the magical girls who passed Cranberry's exams?"

The directness of her statement gave Fal pause for about two seconds. "No, pon." Then, "If the purpose of gathering the magical girls who passed Cranberry's exams was punishing them, there would be a number of easier ways to do it, pon. The point of this game was to get them together and test to see if they were really worthy of continuing as magical girls…or that's what it was supposed to be, pon."

"Hmph. I see. Then…what about Lazuline? Even after all our memories were restored, she said she'd never heard of the Musician of the Forest, Cranberry."

"Huh? Hold on. What do you mean, pon?" Fal had no facial expressions, and scattering scales was the only means the hologram had of conveying feeling. But the mascot's voice had gone shrill. "Lazuline didn't know the Musician of the Forest, Cranberry, pon?"

"Listen, Fal. Though I'm sure it's unlikely, just in case, could you check with the master for me?" Pfle was the only one there who was calm. With a hand in her hair, she twirled the ends around her fingers, brought the curls in front of her eye patch, and held them up to the sunlight. Could she see what she was doing? "You didn't bring Lazuline in because you mistook the current one for the old one, did you?" Pfle spread her fingers again to release the hair, and her curl dropped back down. "If someone familiar with the faces of the participants in question had made the selection, I'm sure no errors would have been made. However, if an outsider who didn't participate in the exam selected participants simply based on documents that she'd intercepted, I'm sure she would make mistakes of this nature."

Shadow Gale was surprised. Lazuline hadn't had any connection to Cranberry? This was new information. Had Pfle figured this out based on the fact that Lazuline was the second magical girl by that name, and the fact that she didn't know of Cranberry?

"Personally," Pfle continued, "I do see myself as a victim, though. If the families of the magical girls who died in my exam came and said to me, *You monster! Don't play the victim*, then I'd be unable to refute them. And I can understand the concerns about those like us passing Cranberry's exams and joining the ranks. As an involved party, I'd want to deny such concerns, but objectively speaking, I couldn't really argue… However. How could you bring in an innocent magical girl with no connection whatsoever to those murderous exams? If you tell me that's acceptable, then any justice this game might claim to have is false." Palms up, Pfle faced Fal. "This is cruel, isn't it? What did Lazuline do? There was no reason to force her to participate in this game—and of course, no reason for her to die, either!"

The volume of scales sparking off Fal's body increased. Pfle's tone was increasingly intense. "Is there any point in this game if it lacks justice? No, there is not. Tell that to the master. Tell them to put a swift end to this and release us."

Fal froze. The scattered scales faded and disappeared. "This is a notice from the master, pon. It has been acknowledged that what happened with Lapis Lazuline was an accident, pon."

"How wonderful that she's so gracious about it."

"But having said that, even the master cannot stop a game in progress, pon. The program will not end unless you fulfill the designated completion requirement, pon."

"That's not very convincing." Pfle was talking, but Shadow Gale was not even trying to follow her meaning. She was just watching.

"The rationale for this game has already collapsed. Whether it will be stopped or not is not something for you to decide."

Fal didn't reply, and Pfle continued.

"You dragged in Lazuline, an entirely blameless magical girl, but now you say standard operating procedures prevent you from putting a halt to the game? How very bureaucratic! We're being forced into participating in a game that should have ended long ago." Pfle's voiced echoed in Shadow Gale's skull. She wanted to hold her head and keel over.

Pfle was trying to use Lazuline as a bargaining chip. When Lazuline had first said she didn't know Cranberry, Pfle must have become aware of her position in the game. If Pfle had used Fal to tell the master what she was explaining now, then maybe Lazuline wouldn't have had to die. But even knowing what she did, Pfle hadn't done anything.

Something was swirling around inside Shadow Gale's chest. It was black, the color that resulted from mixing the others together. It was muddied. Even Shadow Gale couldn't see through it.

"I demand...," Pfle began.

Shadow Gale looked at Pfle's back. Her long hair hid most of it. Occasionally, a gust of wind swayed her curls, giving Shadow Gale just a glimpse. Her back was not large at all, but she was poised. Her back conveyed her belief that she was in the right.

"...that you put an end to this game right now!"

"That's not an option for the master anymore, pon. If the Evil King is eliminated, the game will end that instant, pon. Please, defeat the Evil King quickly."

Pfle turned off her phone, and Fal disappeared. That final exchange had made Shadow Gale's face twist. One shallow remark pierced deep into her with terrible violence.

If the Evil King is eliminated, the game will end that instant.

"Hold on, please," said Shadow Gale. "That can't be right. If the Evil King goes away, the game ends immediately. And the Evil King was one of the magical girls here, the one obstructing the game. She was killing a lot of people, right? And you said Melville's head was cut off, didn't you, miss? So then why isn't the game over?" Shadow Gale sensed that for the first time in a very long time, she had been able to snap back at Pfle. It might have been nothing more than a puppy's soft nip, but it was probably the first time she had argued with her since they'd gotten their memories back. Even as Shadow Gale recognized the hints of unease lurking in Pfle's words, she was glad that she'd been able to argue. "Melville did everything, right? Melville was the Evil King?"

"I...*did* think that Melville was the Evil King," Pfle replied.

"I mean, she was, right? You said so, didn't you?"

"I believed that assassinating the other players was something only the Evil King would do."

"Nobody but the Evil King would have done that," Shadow Gale said.

"This means that while she was the most likely candidate, she was not, in fact, the Evil King. If she were, then the game would already be over. So therefore, she was not the Evil King but just a player who went around killing the others. I can only speculate as to her motives for such violence, but judging from her costume, I can imagine. Essentially, she wanted a killing match."

"There's no way..."

"I won't entirely discard the possibility that Melville is the Evil King. She may have used her magic to camouflage herself to make Clantail believe she'd cut off her head...but that wouldn't explain why Nokko was burned to death." She had left their ranks without a word, and then someone had burned her to cinders. The murder weapon was probably the flamethrower sold in the Evil King's castle. No other weapon could kill someone like that.

"What we need to do," said Pfle, "is prepare ourselves for anyone to be the Evil King."

"What if we get killed before we're ready?"

"I've already taken care of that." Pfle turned on her magical phone. "Those doll remains and the tiny girl who looked like Rionetta...that was most likely Rionetta's real body. Do you recall that there was a magical phone lying beside her where she fell?

When I checked it, I found multiple travel passes inside. If the owner of that phone was the one managing noncombat items, we can assume it was Pechka's. Though it if it was Rionetta's, that would be fine, too. I took the travel passes from that phone, as well as the number of travel passes in circulation since we arrived at the Evil King's castle. The only passes in circulation are the ones you and I possess."

"What about Clantail's?"

"Passes are shared among a party, since they're used on the party unit. Rionetta or Pechka must have been managing them all."

"And what about Nokko and Lazuline?" Shadow Gale asked.

"I've been managing our party's passes."

"And Melville?"

"Judging from the number of passes in circulation right now and the number of passes we hold, she has zero. Being that all that's left of Melville is a severed head, her body must have been horribly damaged in battle, and her magical phone destroyed along with it." Pfle summoned up their item list and showed it to Shadow Gale. The number for the travel passes was on the display: an unbelievable 10,000 (10,000). The maximum number for the travel passes was ten thousand, and the number of passes in circulation was also ten thousand, so no more could be purchased. Pfle grinned boldly. "I bought them all. The passes lose effect a day after use, but they're not depleted if they're never used. Now no one but us can travel between areas."

It would have required an incredible amount of magical candy in order to monopolize the travel passes. There was no way you could gather that much by diligently hunting monsters and finishing quests. Shadow Gale had been the one to gather that candy. The amount used to buy up all those passes was only a fraction of Shadow Gale's earnings. She had gathered that much candy through her grinding efforts.

When Masked Wonder's Miracle Coin had been stolen, Fal had told them that if an event item goes out of circulation, the event will recur. Pfle had zeroed in on that rule. By selling the Dragon

Shield won through defeating the Great Dragon, they had revived the dragon to defeat it again. You could easily make a fortune in magical candy by repeating this over and over.

Fighting the normal way, they never would have been able to defeat the Great Dragon with just the two of them, but there was a way to get around that. Pfle had most likely realized it before they'd even fought the dragon. Right in the middle of the fight, Shadow Gale had looked at Melville attacking the dragon from outside the red line and figured it out. If you attacked from outside the red line, you could defeat it safely without ever giving it a chance.

But neither Pfle nor Shadow Gale had any weapons or abilities that would enable them to attack from a distance like Clantail's spears, Melville's javelins, Daisy's beam, the samurai girl's slash, or Lazuline's teleportation. Pfle's high-powered wheelchair with its built-in killer laser had already been destroyed.

Pfle had ordered Shadow Gale to modify the toy bow and arrow they'd acquired through *R*, and she'd made it into a large, mounting-style firing device. Its ammunition was the Dragon-Killer dagger. As long as it hit, it could kill any dragon in one strike, no matter how massive the beast. If she missed, she just had to return the Dragon-Killer to her magical phone by canceling the item summon.

Pfle had spent some of the magical candy they'd stored up via this method to buy up all of *R*. With *R*, the rarer the item, the lower the drop rate, but even the most common item, the map, had a circulation limit. Once the total stock of maps hit the maximum, you would no longer receive a map from a pull. By sheer force of wealth, they had acquired all the *R* items with their massive abundance of candy.

The items acquired through *R* were mostly just mundane objects and not the sort that would meet Pfle's standards, so she zeroed in on something else. Even mundane items could become weapons if Shadow Gale modified them, like the toy bow and arrow she had transformed into the large firing device.

Pfle tossed a plethora of these mundane items out of her magical phone, telling Shadow Gale to go on and modify them.

"This is too much," said Shadow Gale.

"We're going to do it anyway. We don't have that much time left."

"We do have time, don't we? I mean, no one can travel now, right?"

"Only for the next two days. Then there will be the premaintenance period event."

Shadow Gale gasped. For the premaintenance event, all the surviving magical girls would be forcibly summoned to the square. Whether or not they had travel passes, they would be forced to come face-to-face.

"We're both the noncombat magical girls. If the Evil King is a fighting magical girl, we'll be unable to strike back, and we'll die. But if we can equip ourselves now, we'll have a chance at victory. With your skills, it must work out somehow. First, let's finish this job."

For the next two days, Shadow Gale poured all her effort into creating weapons. She wouldn't call it "being worked like a slave" because Pfle was helping her out and following her directions. She managed to create a number of weapons, not because she'd gotten a helper, but because she was pushed by necessity and pressed for time. She managed this feat in spite of her client tormenting her with the unreasonable demand that she "should have an easier time of this, compared to the ten-legged tank."

Most of these weapons were based on the stun gun.

The two mini-boss enemies in the Evil King's castle, the knight and the robot, had filled out the end of the monster encyclopedia. There were no evil-type monsters anywhere, but for some reason, the shop sold a stun gun and a flamethrower, which were especially effective against evil-type monsters.

"At the very end of the game, you get to the shop in the Evil King's castle, and it's selling useless joke items? It's difficult to believe. But if you took these items at face value, you should first consider the kind of enemies a weapon such as a stun gun would be used against. Yes, it's for use on humans. So if the description says this weapon is especially effective against evil-type enemies, that must mean an evil-type enemy could only be one of us magical girls." Pfle stated her thoughts and proposed that Shadow Gale should base most of the weapons on the stun gun and flamethrower. The stun gun was a self-defense weapon used to incapacitate opponents, while the flamethrower could only be used for killing. If Shadow Gale had to pick one, she had fewer emotional qualms about using the stun gun.

"Indeed, Mamori. But since I last confirmed the number in circulation, someone else has already bought another flamethrower. The enemy may not necessarily be as kind as you, Mamori, so keep that in mind."

In the end, Shadow Gale used a flamethrower, too.

As they worked on their project, as Shadow Gale gave Pfle instructions and listened to Pfle's requests, no unpleasant thoughts floated up in her mind, and she was able to converse naturally with her partner. Maybe they were just so immersed in the work, she didn't have the time to worry about anything else.

It was the third day since their last login, the day of the pre-maintenance event. Both Shadow Gale and Pfle were on the Evil King's castle terrace, quietly waiting for the time to come. Pfle was on her magic carpet, and so was Shadow Gale. Not sitting but kneeling and ready to jump off and go at any time. Pfle was sitting, as per usual.

The two of them were still and silent as the time passed. All that came into the shop in the Evil King's castle was the occasional breeze blowing through. The scissors and wrench hanging from Shadow Gale's belt rattled and swayed, creating the only sounds. The one thing changing was her mounting anxiety.

Their magical phones broke the silence with the message alert noise. Abruptly, their surroundings went dark.

An event is now beginning. Players, please gather in the square in the wasteland town.

They were transferred from the Evil King's castle, with its stark whiteness and wafting sweet scent, to the wasteland town square, with its plain palette of gray, ocher, brown, and khaki. The transfer was sudden and casual; before Shadow Gale knew it, she was somewhere else. No nausea or rattling of her brain.

The wasteland town plaza was a plaza in name only. It was hushed and desolate.

No, that's not right. Shadow Gale mentally corrected herself. During the very first event, she would have found all the magical girls gathered together to be a magnificent sight. It would be more accurate to say that the place seemed desolate during events now that their numbers had diminished. Back during the first event, there had been fifteen people, and now there were only three.

—Three people.

Pfle, Shadow Gale, and one more.

Shadow Gale looked around. The square was surrounded by buildings. With fifteen girls here, it had felt small. With three, it was huge. There was no cover. Just a broken-down fountain with a mermaid statue decorating it. The fountain was dry, and instead of water, a thin layer of sandy buildup was inside. Everything about this place was just as it had been the last time. No matter how many times they came here, it was the same. Shadow Gale looked around once more. There was no sign of anyone but the three of them.

She looked at the locator device in her hand. She'd turned a thermometer they'd acquired through *R* into a "superthermometer" with the added functionality of the map application that told them their party members' locations. Pfle had teased her about the name she'd given it, calling it tasteless, but its functionality was no joke. It was a fantastic item that could be used to detect the surface temperature of objects and display them on the screen. Pfle had made her build it in a hurry, saying that if worse came to worst and Melville was still alive, they would be in real trouble without it.

According to the superthermometer, there were only three magical girls in the square.

"There's no one else." She tried saying it out loud. Nobody replied.

Pfle looked around cautiously and activated her magical phone. It lit up, sparkled, and a holographic image appeared. "Now then, about the event this time. The Miracle Coin contest will recur—"

"Hold on," Pfle said to Fal.

"What is it, pon?"

"I've asked this before, but I want to confirm this with you one more time. There's no way to avoid the forced transportation to the premaintenance period event, correct?"

"No, pon. The players are forcibly summoned for the premaintenance period event, and all magical girls in the game, no matter who, will be gathered in the plaza, pon. If they don't reach it in time, they will be forcibly teleported, pon."

Pfle turned her head ninety degrees to the side and then faced forward again. It seemed she was scanning the area.

"By the way, what are you doing, pon?" asked Fal.

Shadow Gale was on Pfle's magic carpet, too, just in case the Evil King, who'd been stuck in the wasteland area, had set traps in the square in preparation for the premaintenance period event while Pfle and Shadow Gale had been arming themselves. Shadow Gale was probably the only one of all the girls who would have been able to make explosive or electrical mechanical traps, but anyone could dig a pit.

But it seemed Fal's question was not just about that, but also about their weapons. It was judging them for the arsenal Shadow Gale had procured. "Hey, hold on… Why has it come to this, pon? Obviously, the stun gun was being sold in the Evil King's castle with the intention of making the magical girls fight one another in the final stages, pon. And the master also came up with the nasty idea of including a flamethrower so you all wouldn't object to using the stun gun instead, pon. Why would you use something like that? It's just what the master wants, pon."

"None of your business. Shut your trap." Shadow Gale dropped her magical phone on the ground and stepped on it with her toe to turn it off. Fal's words were rumbling like an earthquake in her chest, and she felt like the pain would rip her apart. She didn't want to hear this.

"I'd like to ask one thing," said Pfle.

Yes. What Shadow Gale wanted to know was something else.

"Are you the Evil King?" she asked the magical girl standing on the opposite side of the fountain.

Today, she was a horse. Under the rays of the sun pouring into the square, Shadow Gale could see her robust musculature and beautiful coat, even at this distance. Her human upper body held a spear in its right hand, while in her left, she held a shield at the ready. Her horse's tail swiped up to smack her rear.

"No." Clantail's reply was short and brief. She shot back an equally short, brief question. "What happened to Nokko?"

"She was killed," said Pfle. "What happened to Pechka, Lazuline, and Melville?"

"Melville killed Pechka and Lazuline..." Clantail looked down as if in pain. "...And I killed Melville." She raised her head sharply and glared at Pfle.

Pfle was calm. "You killed Melville? That's impressive." Clantail didn't reply. Pfle continued, her tone casual. "Fal told me that if the Evil King dies, the game will end immediately."

"...I've heard the same thing."

Shadow Gale recalled how Pfle had tried to use Lazuline as bargaining chip, and pain pricked deep in her heart. Everything she'd forgotten for the two days she'd been working on those weapons in the Evil King's castle came back to her.

"I killed Melville, so why isn't the game over?!" Clantail cried out in frustration.

In a voice that was calm but resonant, Pfle replied, "It must be that Melville was not the Evil King."

"Then it's one of you two."

"Neither of us is the Evil King. In other words, Clantail, *you* have to be the Evil King."

The argument across the fountain and the fifty-foot-wide gap between them stopped for a moment. Clantail raised a leg and stamped the ground with a hoof. The kick was hard enough to shake the whole square and leave a deep impression on the ground. "I'm *not* the Evil King."

"That's just what the Evil King would say," Pfle countered.

"Why were all the travel passes sold out? I couldn't buy any."

"Because I bought them all. We couldn't have the Evil King coming into our area."

"How did you get so much candy? You'd need fifty thousand to buy up all the travel passes."

"Our plentiful stores of candy are a result of legitimate in-game efforts."

"Because you're the Evil King?"

"That hardly warrants an accusation."

Clantail jumped. Her horse legs bent to build power, and then she leaped. A kick of her hoof, and the head of the mermaid statue adorning the fountain was shooting toward them. Shadow Gale blocked the head with the Dragon Shield, but Clantail was already looming in front of them.

Shadow Gale and Pfle split to the left and right. As she jumped to the side, Shadow Gale swung at Clantail with her wrench in an attempt to hold her back, but Clantail smacked upward with her shield and knocked it away behind Shadow Gale. Shadow Gale's hand tingled. When Clantail followed her shield blow with a hoof, Shadow Gale somehow managed to block it with her own Dragon Shield. Even though her equipment was +12, the impact lifted her off the ground. Fortunately, her shield hand was not numbed.

From behind Clantail, Pfle thrust out a stun gun weapon. This one had been modified using a bamboo stick. It had far greater reach than the original stun gun, and it was flexible, too. Clantail slipped past the difficult-to-avoid attack by transforming her lower body into a snake and whipping her tail to hit Pfle behind her. Pfle blocked the tail-strike with her shield, but couldn't absorb the full impact. She fell from her carpet and tumbled along the ground.

The difference in skill between combat and noncombat magical girls, as Pfle had put it, was clear to them. Even in a two-on-one fight, Clantail was insanely strong.

Clantail's lower body transformed into a yellowish-brown creature with a tawny pattern and long legs—so long that she blocked out the sun. A giraffe. She raised up her spear. Shadow Gale was about to use her shield to block, but then a shiver of fear ran up her spine. The tip of Clantail's spear rose up, sparkling, reflecting the sunlight from high in the heavens. Shadow Gale looked up, tossed away her shield on the hunch that this wasn't going to work, and jumped to the side.

Clantail's spear swung down, and as it did, she transformed from a giraffe into a tiger to increase the speed and power of her strike. Her spear sliced deep into the earth, making the ground shake. Even though it had to be just a weapon +7, with Clantail swinging it, even Shadow Gale's Shield +12 couldn't block it entirely. The wall that was the difference between their combat capabilities loomed grimly over Shadow Gale.

Clantail then spun around to slash her spear horizontally at Pfle, who had climbed onto her magic carpet again and was pressing in on Clantail from behind. Pfle lowered the height of her carpet and flattened herself down to evade the strike. It sliced off some of her hair, and her golden curls floated away and scattered.

For the first time, Clantail's back was to Shadow Gale. Clantail's back was broad and respectable. It seemed reliable somehow, in a different manner from Pfle's. Seeing her back, something inside Shadow Gale's heart whispered. Could a back that had shouldered the underhanded role of the Evil King be so dignified? Was Clantail really the Evil King?

Shadow Gale shook off the whispers and threw the net. This was an electromagnetic mesh that could cover a wide area. She'd made it by combining a rope from *R* with a stun gun. If she flung this at Clantail from behind, even she would have a hard time avoiding it.

She caught her target in the net, and before Clantail had even a moment to struggle, she was electrocuted. The stun gun could knock out a magical girl in one zap. Clantail's knees hit the ground, and her head slumped. Shadow Gale was letting her guard down, thinking the fight was over, when the butt of Clantail's spear came toward her.

Clantail was thrusting back without looking behind, and the

handle of her spear skimmed Shadow Gale's arm. It wasn't a direct hit, but it split open the flesh of her right arm in a spurt of blood. An awful sound came from her bone. Shadow Gale screamed and clutched her wounded arm. Clantail turned around.

Clantail's eyes were burning with anger. On her chest, a necklace flashed. It was a charm sold at one of the shops…the earth charm. It conferred resistance to lightning-elemental attacks.

Shadow Gale understood why the electrical net hadn't worked. Clantail would just have had to peek at the item encyclopedia to know that someone had bought a large number of stun guns. So all she had to do was equip herself with the accessory that would give her resistance to electricity. That was the earth charm Clantail was wearing.

Faster than Clantail could swing down her spear, Pfle attacked Clantail from behind, and Clantail turned around to block with her shield. They both went in to swing at each other and dodge their respective hits.

Shadow Gale's heart was still whispering. *Did you see Clantail's eyes just now? That wasn't just anger. There was sadness there, too. That wasn't the look of someone who fights knowing she's the Evil King.*

Shadow Gale countered the voice inside her. There were only three people left: herself, Pfle, and Clantail. The Evil King had to be Clantail.

Even as she argued with herself, in her heart, she was smoldering. It was suspicion. She couldn't rid herself of her misgivings, and she couldn't stop thinking about Cranberry's exam. It would be easy enough for Pfle to deceive her. She would lure Shadow Gale in, and the two of them would defeat Clantail together. Once that was done, Pfle would finish Shadow Gale off, now that her job was over, and Pfle would be the last girl standing.

"Mamoriii!" Pfle's yell snapped her back to reality. Clantail was pushing Pfle back. Pfle had pulled out the flamethrower, and it was gushing flames, but Clantail blocked with her shield and swiped them aside with her spear, deftly avoiding any direct hits. Shadow

Gale picked up her wrench and approached Clantail, but Clantail wouldn't have that, transforming into an alligator to whip her tail at Shadow Gale and keep her at bay.

But now her upper body was positioned lower to the ground. Pfle hopped casually down from her carpet. For just a moment, Clantail froze. Pfle hadn't stood once, up until this point. She had either been riding her wheelchair or the magic carpet, or Shadow Gale had been carrying her. Shadow Gale knew—Pfle could walk normally. She just avoided revealing that to others as much as possible. And then, at times like these, she could catch people off guard by suddenly standing up.

Now that Clantail had given her an opening, Pfle took full advantage. Bounding off the ground, she grabbed Clantail's shield hand. Clantail jerked her shield from side to side to throw Pfle off and flung her away together with the shield. Pfle spun in the air and landed gently on all fours.

A greasy sweat was breaking out on Clantail's forehead. Her left hand, the one that had been holding the shield, was now shaking. Her little and ring fingers were broken, pointing in the wrong directions. Pfle had fought in just the same way back then, too. She would pretend that she couldn't walk to deceive the weak, and when the time came, she would hop up and attack. Her opponents would be stunned, and Pfle would injure them, just as she had done with Clantail.

Yes, Cranberry's exam. It was just like back then. Something black was swirling around inside Shadow Gale. It was hot, muddy, and slowly increasing in volume.

Was the Evil King really Clantail?

Wasn't it Pfle who was the Evil King?

Just now, Pfle had judged based on process of elimination that since neither Shadow Gale nor Pfle were the Evil King, then it had to be Clantail. But how could Pfle say for certain that Shadow Gale wasn't the Evil King? Maybe she had slipped and revealed her position as the Evil King. It Pfle herself were the Evil King, she would know Shadow Gale was not—that was self-explanatory.

Pfle blasted some more flames, and Clantail transformed into a leopard to nimbly evade them. Her dodge took her right to where the Dragon Shield lay, where Shadow Gale had dropped it. Clantail swiftly scooped it up and held it with her intact pointer and middle fingers and thumb.

This was part of their strategy, too. Before the battle had begun, Shadow Gale had deliberately thrown away her magical phone. Doing this meant Shadow Gale could no longer de-summon items and return them to her magical phone, creating a situation where it was possible for her items to be stolen. And the Dragon Shield, with its +12 modification, was an item worth stealing.

Pfle pulled a remote control out of her sleeve and pressed it. Flames spewed out from the *inside* of the Dragon Shield. Clantail screamed voicelessly, throwing away the shield and writhing in pain. Her lower body transformed into a massive, translucent jellyfish, which wrapped around her flaming upper body. Shadow Gale had heard before that a jellyfish's body was mostly made up of water. Clantail sizzled, and steam was rising from her body as she put out the flames, but she was still horribly burned. She curled up, moaning.

Shadow Gale had seen this exact same thing many times before during Cranberry's exam. Pfle's plots, traps, and trickery had done in countless magical girls, leaving their bodies sprawled on the ground.

And in this game, she had been the same. Pfle had announced Masked Wonder's murder in the square and arranged for all the girls to face the Great Dragon at once just to see their reactions, and in both cases, that had caused an outbreak of chaos. But even when people died, Pfle had no regrets.

Only Pfle had known when Nokko ran off. It was odd, and Shadow Gale didn't even really know why she had died. Might Pfle have been able to kill Nokko? Most people wouldn't be able to. But Pfle…

Shadow Gale picked up her wrench in her left hand and surged forward. The black, muddy stream in her heart was at a rolling boil, whirling around and around in circles. She had to do it. This was her only chance. The more the current rushed around, the faster it got, the hotter it got, the bigger it got, the muddier and blacker it got. Shadow Gale charged toward Pfle and swung the wrench at her face.

Pfle had been focused on Clantail's writhing, and she would never have dreamed that she would be attacked from the side. She didn't avoid or block the strike, and Shadow Gale got a solid hit. She felt it connect. The sound, the sensation of breaking bones, all of it was telling her inside her heart that she had done it right. Pfle soared away and landed on her back on the road that led from the square, rolling and sliding along the ground until she finally reached a stop.

Shadow Gale was watching Pfle. She'd been watching her steadily, right up until the moment she'd swung that wrench into her face. If Pfle was the Evil King, then she would have to react somehow. She might be angry or upset, or she could be trying to deceive Shadow Gale. Shadow Gale had to get to the bottom of this. *Come on, how will you react? You won't deceive me anymore.*

Pfle lay face-up on the ground. Her fingers twitched twice, then stopped. In Shadow Gale's heart, the black torrent transformed into swirling exultation.

Shadow Gale couldn't believe that Clantail was the Evil King. And she didn't understand how Pfle could have trusted Shadow Gale so blindly. Every single thing she had done had been suspicious. Her claim that she would make judgments based on character had just been an excuse for her to ignore Melville, hadn't it? After all, the Evil King would be glad to have such a capable individual going around killing off the others on her own.

Shadow Gale looked at her left hand. Gripping the wrench, it was trembling.

She looked at Pfle. She wasn't even twitching now. Chills shot down Shadow Gale's spine. It couldn't be. With one hit?

What am I doing?

I've killed Pfle? Killed her? Why? Why would I?

She recalled her parents saying that they'd named her Mamori so that she would protect her young mistress. Her knees weakened.

She couldn't stand. She'd killed Kanoe. She'd killed Kanoe. But...it wasn't over. The game wasn't over yet.

Strength drained from her legs, Shadow Gale was on her way to the ground when something came in from behind to support her. It was a hand grabbing her collar to lift her up.

"You're...the Evil King, huh?" It was Clantail. She still had some burns, but the majority of them had healed. Her left hand, the one holding Shadow Gale, didn't seem to be wounded, either. She'd clearly used a recovery medicine.

"The Evil King...?" Shadow Gale wanted to deny it, but the words wouldn't come out. It wasn't that she was scared of Clantail. She was terrified of herself for having been so driven by her suspicions that she had struck Pfle down. Tears began to spill out from her eyes as if they'd burst through a dam.

Clantail's right hand adjusted its grip on her spear. "Lazuline and Pechka saved me... I can't die." That meant, *I can't die; I'm sorry, but I'm going to kill you.* Clantail was announcing that she would end Shadow Gale's life. Pfle was dead, and only Clantail and Shadow Gale were left, so the Evil King had to be Clantail now.

The wrench slipped from Shadow Gale's hand. Her hand felt weak. The weapon felt disgusting to her. She could still feel the sensation of Pfle's skull breaking.

Everything rapidly faded inside her. She didn't care anymore what happened.

"I've got it!" A very familiar voice called out, and Shadow Gale winced in shock. Clantail was stunned, too. Both of them looked over to the road where Pfle had landed to see the owner of the voice pushing her upper body off the ground. "I get it. I've figured it out. What frightening magic."

Pfle sat up entirely, observing Shadow Gale and Clantail. Pfle's nose had been severely crushed, and her face was soaked in blood. Her face—which was especially beautiful, even for a magical girl—was entirely ruined. But there was still light in her eyes. Perhaps the strength in them overwhelmed Clantail, as she retreated half a step.

"When I considered who might be the Evil King," Pfle said, "I excluded the possibility that it was you, Mamori. I was confident about that judgment, but not entirely certain. I figured I wouldn't really mind if you were the Evil King. Even if it was you, things would work out as long as I conducted myself in such a way as to put you at an advantage. It didn't matter to me if you were the Evil King or a player. As long as you survived, that was enough for me. If you were the Evil King, I would have cooperated with you in killing the other players."

Clantail let go of Shadow Gale, who hit the ground on her bottom and moaned in pain.

With no apparent concern, Pfle continued. "But...then something strange happened. At some point, I came to think that perhaps I shouldn't be trusting you, Mamori. Before then, I'd been willing to go along with anything as long as you were with me. So what kind of situation would make me feel like I couldn't trust you anymore? Although I found this baffling, I continued to be suspicious of you...until just now, when you knocked me down. You hit me, I flew back, I rolled along the ground, and then all the doubts building in my heart faded away."

Shadow Gale put her hands on the ground and inched back farther. She didn't understand what Pfle was saying. She couldn't understand. But she couldn't stop crying, regardless.

Slowly, Pfle stood. "It's strange, isn't it? I was suspicious of you to begin with, and then you hit me hard enough to knock me away. You'd expect that to convince me that you were the enemy, but that blow dispelled my misgivings. Clearly, there was something wrong with my head. What had caused this? As I looked up at the sky, I thought about it. Now that the strange suspicion was gone, I could think again. Yes. It was the square. My suspicions went away because I was out of the plaza."

Pfle stepped from the road into the square. "It's just as I thought. When I enter this area, my heart clouds. I feel suspicious, and my mind becomes dull. Something is preventing me from questioning the situation. It's making me avert my eyes from things that I normally would've considered. And these effects aren't just limited to myself. It's affecting everyone in this place. Mamori, trust Clantail. She's not the Evil King."

Once more, Shadow Gale heard whispering in her heart. *Don't listen to what she's saying. She's a master of trickery. If you listen to her, you'll lose.*

"Mamori! Don't get distracted!" Blood was pouring and gushing from Pfle's crushed nose like a waterfall. But her voice still carried from the road into the square, striking into Shadow Gale's chest, too. The whispers scattered and dispersed, and the black torrent instantly evaporated.

"Both of you, come over here! And under no condition do you let your guard down!" Pfle stood in front of the fountain. She and Clantail looked at each other and then nodded together. Shadow Gale raised the Dragon Shield and a stun gun while Clantail transformed her lower body into a tiger. Both of them headed toward either side of the fountain.

"There's sand piled up here," said Pfle. "We're going to clear it all away. Be ready—we could be attacked at any moment." They obeyed her. All three of them scooped the sand out from the fountain until it was empty.

"Here, look. Do you see anything odd here?" Pfle asked. They had exposed the bottom of the fountain. And indeed, there was an unnatural crack there, a circular fissure about three feet in diameter. "Break it open!"

Clantail raised her front legs and swung them down. Since the middle was already cracked, the bottom of the fountain split easily, and fragments of stone fell away. There was a space underneath.

Shadow Gale slowly leaned over, peering into the space. Under the fountain was a hole about seven feet squared, and inside it was a girl in a maid outfit holding her right wrist, trembling.

☆ **Nokko**

In this game, you will take on the role of the Evil King.

* * *

That was what was written in the message sent to Nokko's magical phone. Her win condition was the death of all other players.

If you watched the entire chain of incidents Cranberry had caused from above, Nokko would have clearly been classified as an aggressor, not a victim. She had once been a member of a group of magical girls whose leader had been a Cranberry sympathizer. Nokko had received compensation many times in exchange for cooperating with exams. Her role had been to induce action in the more reluctant magical girls. She would approach the participants, pretending to be a normal person, and transmit anger, hatred, and other feelings to them to speed up the exam.

She hadn't been in a position to know everything about the exams. But still, she'd had a general grasp on what she was doing. While she'd known it wasn't a good thing, she'd continued to cooperate because she wanted the money. Ever since Nokko's father had vanished, her family had needed money. Normally, you couldn't make any money being a magical girl. So she had no choice but to earn it through abnormal means.

When Nokko's group leader had been exposed as Cranberry's coconspirator, she had been brought to justice, and Nokko had lost her source of income. But the authorities of the Magical Kingdom had not touched Nokko. Her leader might have covered for her. Though she'd felt bad, she had been relieved.

But the master of *Magical Girl Raising Project* knew what Nokko had done. The master had come to her, telling her that either they would expose everything, or she could participate in this game. She had to pick one.

Nokko's old leader was still missing, and Nokko couldn't go off and leave her mother. She didn't have any options.

But when the time came to actually start the game, Nokko joined the others in playing it. All the others had gotten themselves worked up about how they could end the game if they just defeated the Evil King, but Nokko hadn't been given that information. Her win condition was different from that of all the others.

The game progressed, and she never told anyone who she was. When she had found out that death in the game meant death in the real world, she'd sunk into a deep despair. Would these forced games of kill-or-be-killed never end?

Nokko thought about just confessing instead. If she alone were to die, then all the others would be saved. But she couldn't do it. Her mother's face rose in her mind. And while she was busy waffling, the other magical girls were dying. Not in accidents like Magical Daisy. Someone was killing them.

A number of the magical girls participating in this game were those Nokko had seen during Cranberry's exams. Nokko had more information than the others, so slowly, she came to understand what the master was trying to do. Those who had been involved with Cranberry were being checked to see if they were the right material. Nokko, who had been a part of Cranberry's plots, was being given one last chance.

She had no choice but to take that chance and run with it.

Whenever she had the chance to encounter other magical girls during events and such, Nokko spread the seeds of discord. She encouraged the conflict between Rionetta and Nonako. She urged on Melville, made Pechka more frightened, and made Shadow Gale suspicious of Pfle. But she conducted herself with the utmost caution so that she would never become the target of their hatred and anger.

Even with their memories gone, the magical girls who had gone through the exams still had darkness and wounds in their hearts. Nokko's magic worked well on people like that.

When Nokko had heard that Melville's crimes had been exposed, she'd figured that as the Evil King, she could end this soon without doing a thing. Using @Meow-Meow's body and a flamethrower, she had faked her own death. She'd burned up the corpse while intoning, *I'm sorry, I'm sorry* like a spell, and then cut off her own hand, sobbing with pain and shock, and incinerated that, too.

After that, she had just waited until the premaintenance period event. She'd used the shovel to make a space under the fountain to hide and then transmitted feelings to the magical girls who gathered there. She'd turned their attention away from her so that they wouldn't notice her hiding spot while she spread negative feelings of suspicion, hate, and anger. She would induce them to kill one another, and in the survivor, she would induce a deep, deep despair to make her kill herself.

In order to be the last one, Nokko had no other choice. But now she'd failed, and she'd ruined her last chance. The three magical girls outside the hole were looking down at Nokko.

The three magical girls were standing with the sun at their backs. Nokko couldn't detect in their expressions any sense of superiority as the victors or joy at having finished the game. As they gazed down at Nokko, Shadow Gale, Clantail, and even Pfle seemed somehow sad.

No. Not yet. There was still one more thing she could do. She had one chance left.

Hands shaking, Nokko brought out a magical phone and threw it away. She'd abandoned her own magical phone, so the one she was using was @Meow-Meow's. She'd acquired it from digging up her grave.

She took the shovel in her left hand. The shovel's sharp tip had helped her dig many holes, and it had also helped her with splitting open the bottom of the fountain. This shovel, the one that Clantail had given her, had not chipped once, right to the end.

Nokko smiled at the trio. She couldn't stop herself from shaking, no matter what, but still, she tried to give them a brave smile. "I'm not going to resist. But...will you make a deal with me?"

MASTER SIDE #11

One block of the cube changed color. The game was over.

As if she'd been waiting for that, Show White opened her mouth. "Tell me one thing." It was the first time she'd spoken since entering the room.

That proposal definitely moved her heart. The girl chuckled.

"I heard there was one magical girl who was unconnected to any of this."

"Oh, that. Something Lazuline, was it? The real confusing one? I gueeess you could say she wasn't involved. And well, I won't deny that it was my mistake that inadvertently led to her participation. But she still received training from one of the children, you know? I guess we could call her semi-involved, eh? Well, she did do some pretty crazy fighting mid-game before she died, so I'd say no problem there. Ha-ha." She laughed.

Snow White narrowed her eyes silently.

"So anyway. Who cares about that stuff? Join me, Snow White. Lots of Cranberry's children are still out there. Let's screen them, the two of us together. You and me are sure to do a good job. We'll create a world that only has righteous magical girls." The girl leaned forward on the desk and took Snow White's hand. Snow White nodded silently, and the girl returned her nod with an enormous grin.

"I understand that Cranberry's children are dangerous," said Snow White.

"Yeah! Right? I thought you'd understand!"

"The magical girls chosen by the killing exams are selfish and egotistical. When things don't go as they want, they try to solve things with violence. And in order to enact what they think is right, they'll even oppose the Magical Kingdom's orders…and I'm that way, too."

"No way!" The girl squeezed Snow White's hand tighter. "You're different, Snow White! You didn't kill anyone, and you got Cranberry! Without you, she might still be holding her battle royals!"

"I didn't defeat Cranberry."

"But it happened because you were there." The girl was still grasping Snow White's hand, and she shook it up and down. Both of their hands hit the desk, rattling the saucers and cups.

Snow White's eyes rose to examine the girl. "But other than Cranberry…"

"Hmm?"

"There were examiners other than Cranberry holding killing exams. What about those children?"

"Of course, they get the same treatment as Cranberry's children! The *right* kind of magical girl will be forgiven. I'll never allow the *wrong* kind of magical girl to pass."

"And if those children hold more battle royals?"

"I'd definitely never let that go. I won't let any of those types call themselves magical girls. I'll get rid of them. I won't even need an exam to do that."

Snow White tried to pull her hand away from the girl's grasp. But the girl made no move to let go, so Snow White wrenched it away. "My magic…has changed quite a bit since I first acquired it."

"Huh. So in other words, that means you've grown, huh?"

"It used to be that I could hear the thoughts of people in trouble. The fundamental nature of my magic still hasn't changed, but now I can hear deep psychology, reflexive thought, and even things a person is not aware they're thinking."

"Oh yeah. I saw your fight with Flame-Flamey, and I could kinda tell." No one attacks while consciously thinking, *I'm about to sweep her legs out from under her, so I sure hope she doesn't dodge.* Snow White had attacked and defended as if she could read even Flame-Flamey's reflexive actions.

"But I can't read erased memories," said Snow White. "Which is why I looked into this myself. Do you remember your teacher's name?"

"Of course I remember! My master was a really amazing magical girl." The girl raised her index finger and opened her mouth halfway as if she were about to say something, and then she stared into empty space. Dust danced in the air. She held that same pose for thirty seconds. "...Huh?"

Her master had been an outstanding and righteous magical girl. Cool, cute, and eloquent, she'd taught her what it meant to be a heroine. Her master would risk her own life for justice and shed tears for strangers. The girl admired her, and even now, aspired to be like her. But in spite of that, she couldn't come up with her master's name.

And not just her name. Her face was vague in her mind, too. She'd admired her master so much, so it was strange that they hadn't continued together. Wouldn't the natural choice be for her to try to team up with her master, rather than Snow White? Why had it never occurred to her to join with her own teacher?

The girl racked her brains, but the answers wouldn't come. She just couldn't think of her master's name.

Snow White reached into the cloth pouch hanging from her belt and pulled out a stack of paper. It was about two hundred sheets total on A4-size paper, held together with a bulldog clip. It looked like some sort of document.

"Your master was Pythie. She was influenced by Cranberry, and she had the examinees under her purview kill each other. She was the first magical girl I caught. The documents here...these documents I just collected are a record all the things she did."

"...Huh?" Pythie. Pythie. It sounded familiar. The girl put her hands to her temples and held her head. It ached. She threw her head back, her chair tipped over, and she hit the floor on her back. Her glasses fell off. The clatter of the chair leaning and hitting a monitor reverberated in the emptiness.

"You can do anything here, just like a god, right? You should try digging up your memories. You'll be able to do that if you read these documents…I think."

Her head hurt. Her head hurt. Like it was being squeezed in a vise. Noise crawled into the walls of the room, the furniture, and the air.

"The magical girls chosen by the killing exams are selfish and egotistical. When things don't go as they want, they try to solve things with violence. And in order to enact what they think is right, they'll even oppose the Magical Kingdom's orders…"

No. No. There was no way. She just had to look at the documents, then. She just had to use her almighty powers to investigate and see if there were any mistakes in her memory, any falsifications. Her head hurt. Her head hurt. There was a pixel missing on the ceiling. And another on the floor. The missing pixels were spreading. She couldn't maintain the form of this world.

Snow White stood, picked up the magical phone lying on the floor, and turned it on. "Now then, I'll be asking you about the situation."

"I'll tell you everything I know, pon. But can I make one request, pon?"

"What?"

"I'd really like it if you changed the settings for my sentence endings, pon."

"We can talk it over."

The sound of Snow White's footsteps echoed through the floor into the girl's body. She heard the automatic doors opening, then closing. She had to call out to Snow White, but she couldn't make a sound. Gaps were beginning to appear in every part of this patchwork realm. The girl's soul screamed. The world was going into collapse. The ground at her feet crumbled away, and she fell into the abyss. She would never reach the bottom.

EPILOGUE

There was just the smallest hint of suspicion hidden in the insincere smile of the server who came to take their order. They were probably worried. Possibly out of sheer kindness, or possibly out of the self-interested desire to avoid any problems in their workplace.

Mamori could sympathize with concerns like that. Seeing these two side by side would give anyone cause for concern.

"It's gotten quite a bit colder lately." Despite having said that, the girl was in a short skirt and drinking iced tea through a straw. Kanoe wouldn't drink hot tea when she was out and about, and her reasoning for that was incredibly obnoxious. "The black tea they serve at restaurants is undrinkable, leaving me no choice but to mask the flavor with coldness." They were even out on an open terrace. Kanoe had insisted on this spot because it was sunny today, and she had taken a seat immediately without giving the other two the option of refusing.

The other girl with them was silently sipping on a hot cocoa. Her silence was typical.

Kanoe stood out. Her clothing and accessories—their cost aside—were not really garish. Her makeup was restrained and

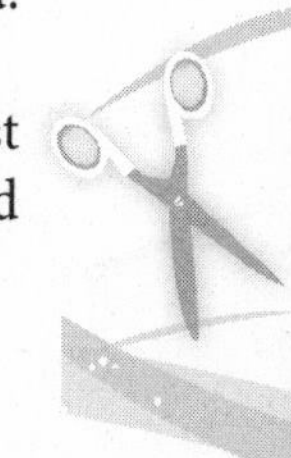

tasteful, too. But her looks, from her luxurious curly hair to her flawless facial features, along with her haughty attitude, prevented Kanoe from being lost in the crowd. Some might say she had an aura, but Mamori thought she was just full of herself.

The other girl with them was extremely plain. She was short—so short she could pass for an elementary school girl. Twin braids hung from either side of her head, her glasses were unfashionable black plastic, and she wore no trace of makeup at all. Her skirt was probably school regulation–length. Her plainness called to mind a bookish nerd or a class president.

They were two entirely different sorts of girl, and you couldn't detect anything they might have in common. It suggested something suspicious was going on between them. Today, all three girls were wearing their school uniforms. Kanoe's and Mamori's uniforms were from the same school. Only the third girl was wearing a different uniform, and she was a middle school student. Mamori couldn't even imagine what sort of assumptions people were making about their group.

Being out on this café's open terrace was making Mamori silently gripe to herself about the cold, but despite the temperature, people started to pour into the café once it hit lunch hour. All the customers led in by servers ended up staring at them. They must have seemed incredibly shady.

"Actually, since the game ended, I've been making some inquiries and talking to people," said Kanoe. Mamori choked a little. "I've tried asking some questions about the master. It seems the Magical Kingdom's negotiator has disposed of them in good order."

"For real? They were dealt with?" said Mamori.

The master had been very literally like a god to them. They had met so many strong magical girls in the game…and some insanely strong ones, too, but even they hadn't been able to touch the master. It wasn't simple helplessness they felt before her. They'd been like ants before a giant. Mamori felt like they'd seen her as some kind of natural phenomenon, like a typhoon or an earthquake.

"Though if they'd been capable of dealing with the master, they really should have done it earlier," said Kanoe.

Clantail—the sober and taciturn middle school girl, Nene Ono—nodded silently.

In order to fulfill her dream of becoming a zoologist, Nene spent every day immersed in study, and she'd also said that recently, she'd begun to study cooking. She didn't seem like a bad girl, but when they'd first met, after Kanoe had revealed herself as Pfle, Nene's expression had said, *I see*. But when Mamori had said she was Shadow Gale, Nene's look had said, *seriously?* And that still bothered Mamori.

While sipping her coffee, Mamori recalled the game's very sudden ending.

They uncovered the space under the fountain and pulled out Nokko, who had been hiding inside. Even though Nokko had manipulated their feelings and tried to force them into a battle to the death, for some reason, Shadow Gale couldn't bring herself to hate her. Looking at the girl trembling under the blaring hot sun, any such emotions vanished.

Nokko was leaning on her shovel, thrust into the earth. Her face was pale, and she was trembling, but Shadow Gale could tell that she was still trying to put on a brave front.

Shadow Gale looked at Clantail. Her expression as a warrior magical girl was now gone, and she was biting her lower lip, shoulders drooping, back slumped as she looked down at Nokko. Even after Clantail had been scorched and had her fingers broken, now that she was on her feet again, she couldn't lay a hand on Nokko.

Pity and sadness seemed to have welled up within Pfle, too. Shadow Gale had known her for a long time, and she'd never seen Pfle look at anyone the way she was looking at Nokko now. They knew if they killed Nokko, the game would be over, but Pfle was still motionless. She looked as if she were desperately racking her brains to try to come up with some other way.

Shadow Gale glanced at the scissors at her waist. She just had to make up her mind, and she could put an end to this game right now…but she didn't want to. She understood Clantail's and Pfle's feelings so well, it hurt.

Nokko spoke, and it sounded as if she was mustering all her willpower and spirit. "Have you…memorized the address and name that was in my magical phone?"

"I have. I won't forget," said Pfle.

Nokko smiled. The smile was small and faint and seemingly on the brink of vanishing, but it left a startlingly deep impression. "Thank you."

"So what's this deal of yours?"

Nokko grabbed the handle of the shovel and pulled it out of the ground. "In exchange for what I'm about to do, send a portion of the reward to that address." She pointed the blade of the shovel at her own throat.

Shadow Gale understood what Nokko was about to do. Nokko could tell that the three of them didn't want to kill her, so she was going to finish the job herself. She was telling them they didn't have to dirty their hands, so they should please give her some of the reward.

Shadow Gale reached out to stop her, but then she pulled her hand back. Right now, even if she did stop Nokko, it would be nothing more than hypocrisy. There was no point.

Shadow Gale looked away. But even with her eyes averted, Nokko's feelings came to her. Shadow Gale's face twisted, and she closed her eyes…then the game ended.

When they returned to the real world, Kanoe seemed sincerely glad, but Mamori was not in the state of mind for that. In fact, what mostly filled her heart was guilt for what she'd done to Kanoe, along with regret. Kanoe said she was just glad Mamori was alive, which made Mamori glad but also even guiltier.

And what was more, when Mamori thought about what had happened in the game, Nokko's end in particular, she couldn't help but feel depressed. After their return, Mamori spent her days just sleeping and waking, sleeping and waking, making the people in her life very concerned. That was when they got ahold of Clantail through the Magical Kingdom.

"Back then, at the end..." Kanoe smiled just a little sadly. "She might have gotten us." Without saying anything more, she put her cup down.

Mamori got the gist of what Kanoe was trying to say. In that moment, neither Clantail, a combat magical girl, nor Pfle the pragmatist had been able to touch Nokko. Thinking back on it, Nokko's magic had to have been affecting their feelings. Even after they'd found her out, Nokko had kept on fighting alone. She'd created a situation where the three of them would have trouble finishing her off so that she could negotiate with them. Then she'd told them she would kill herself for them in exchange for part of the reward.

There were some magical girls who fought, and some who did not. But that didn't mean that the noncombat magical girls were weak.

Nene put down her cup. She was done with her cocoa. Kanoe's tea was long gone, as was Mamori's coffee.

"So then, shall we go?" said Mamori.

"Yes," Kanoe replied. "Let's buy some flowers on the way."

"Do you have any prayer beads?"

"Do you think I'd forget that?" Kanoe replied. "Right then, let's go."

They had twelve graves to visit. Last time, they'd visited two, and they had ten more left to go. One of these visits would include the serious job of somehow giving a large sum of money to a member of Nokko's household. It would be just a bit longer until it was all over.

Afterword

Hello! I'm a magical-girl rice bowl.

This time, it was an unbelievable two-parter! Two grains, enjoyed once... Putting it like that makes it seem like you're somehow losing out, though. But actually, you should think if it as getting to eat twice. Yeah, let's go with that.

The English subtitle for this book, *Restart*, means "to begin again" *Magical Girl Raising Project*, once more. I think it's a wonderful title. I've forgotten who suggested it, but when the decision was made that we would add an English subtitle to the sequel's title, all I could think of was *Magical Girl Raising Project: Pestilence* (fatal infectious disease) or *Magical Girl Raising Project: Vomit* (throwing up). So to me, that subtitle was so resplendent, I couldn't even look straight at it.

Writing a two-parter has changed my work schedule a lot, compared to how it was before. My hobbies and preferences have changed because of it, too. I've come to like three-player mahjong more than four-player. And when I pull a north tile, I don't think, *I pulled a wind tile!* anymore, but *Yes! A* nukidora*!* I've come to love short story collections more than novels. I've become a might-is-right thinker, like *Maybe it's fine if by hunting, hunters*

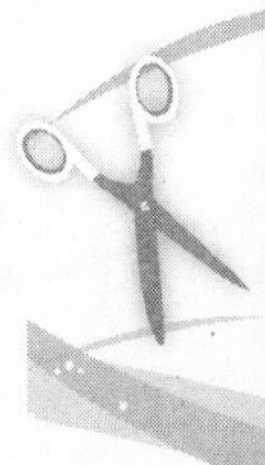

kill all the wolves and foxes. I've become tolerant toward spoilers. I've come to figure that I can push myself on a draft, and it doesn't really matter if it's consistent with the other stuff I'm working on. I've stopped putting Maji-aka on my "psyching myself up" playlist. I've come to enjoy eating things that are easy on my stomach. I'm no longer able to complain about what's on *Iitomo.* My surprise when the Pentagon showed up on the show (Seriously?! That's insane!) probably had nothing to do with this being a two-parter.

A two-parter truly is a fearsome thing, to bring about so many changes.

All righty then, a few more things:

Some things have changed since the completion of Part I, like who I'd planned to have survive and how many girls it would be. You might amuse yourself by trying to deduce who I originally planned to have live to the end. My motto here is to keep everything flexible.

On a phone call to my youngest sister, my other younger sister once said, "Detec Bell is clearly going to die." (I have doubts about my sister for talking about that sort of thing on the phone.) And then her daughter (my niece), heard it and apparently got mad and said, "A magical girl would never die!" I'm sorry. I really am sorry.

To the people of the editorial department who guided me, and to my editor, S-mura-san, who occasionally took jabs at me and occasionally saved me like a holy mother, I give my most gracious thanks. When I sent you a text at five in the morning and you calmly called me back, I got the shivers. Thank you very much.

I also offer great thanks to Marui-no-sensei, who yet again drew such wonderful illustrations for this book. My favorite is the scene where Melville is crushing Pechka underfoot. When I received that illustration, I let out a cry of wonder, making S-mura-san, who was on the phone with me, think something fishy was up.

And finally, to my readers: Thank you very much for purchasing this book. If we have another opportunity, I hope you will take an interest in my future works as well.

I was hoping we could meet again...
and then, while I was finishing
up the previous volume, my wish
came true.
I'm glad I got the chance to
draw this world again.
I was able to decorate
the cover with the nurse
girl, and personally, I'm
satisfied. I succeeded in
my ambitions.
I love nurses, and
I love Shadow Gale,
too.
I love them all.
Thank you so
much!
Marui-no